MW00856093

Atlas of
Paranormal Places

'This book is dedicated to Margaret 'Mrs. Hudson' Paterson — whose death was not the end.'

Atlas of
Paranormal Places

A Journey to the World's
Most Supernatural Places

Evelyn Hollow

Foreword by Danny Robins

IVY PRESS

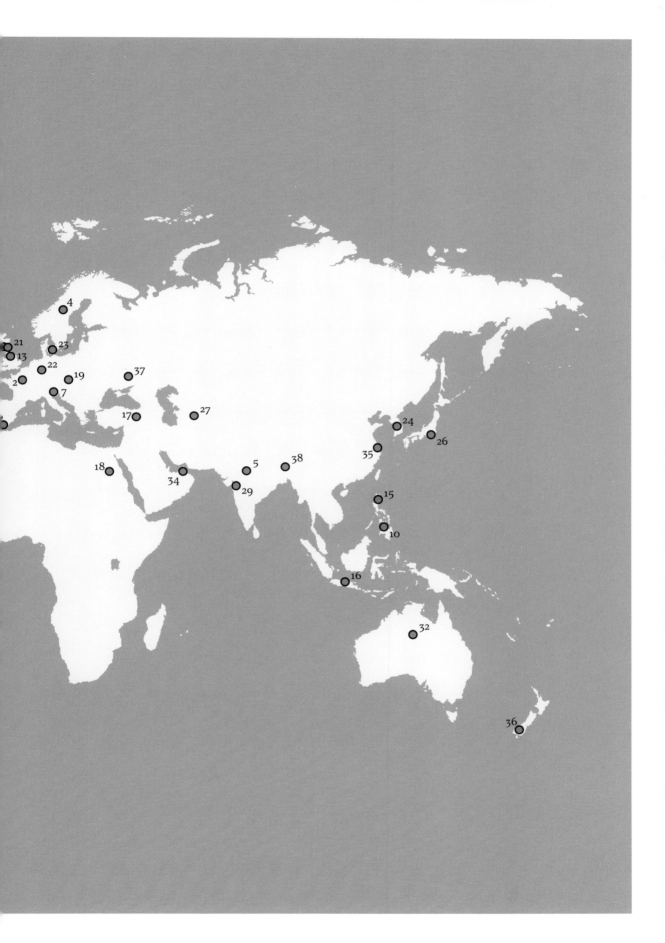

Contents

FIVE – STRANGE NATURE

SIX – CRYPTIDS & CREATURES

Foreword

Are you sitting comfortably? You're sure the room doesn't feel a little chilly despite all the windows being shut? And where's that unaccountable tingle down your spine coming from? Perhaps it's because you are about to dive into a book filled with evocative accounts of some of the (allegedly) most haunted locations in the world, written by one of Britain's foremost experts on the paranormal. I have worked with Evelyn for several years, first on my BBC podcast *The Battersea Poltergeist*, where she broke onto the scene as an engaging, clever, funny and thought-provoking breath of fresh air (a cold breath obviously, this is the paranormal), and then on my further series *The Witch Farm* and *Uncanny*, which also transferred to TV. During this time, I've had the pleasure of watching her grow into one of the most important voices within Britain on this fascinating subject.

The study of the paranormal has not always been taken seriously over the last few decades. Ghost hunting was, at times, considered almost laughable cable-channel entertainment, fuelled by TV shows where people screamed a lot but very little happened. However, humanity's collective itch to scratch never went away; our need to make sense of the strange, sometimes moving, often frightening, things that thousands, if not millions, of people around the world experience. Recently, it feels like there has been a growing renaissance of intelligent debate around wanting to sensibly explore what ghosts might actually be – the products of our minds and environments, or something mind-bogglingly magical – the spirits of the dead.

Evelyn is very much at the forefront of this renaissance, driven to question by her own experiences, but always balanced and reasonable. You don't have to believe ghosts, demons or strange folkloric creatures are real to enjoy this gorgeous, comprehensive book she has written, you just have to take pleasure from the glorious detective story that is our bid to understand the mysteries of human experience; to analyse the moments of our lives that quite literally sit outside the normal.

So, slip on an extra cardigan, pour yourself a stiff drink if that's your poison, or add an extra teabag to that herbal tea, because you are about to embark on a thrilling, spine-tingling journey. Evelyn has curated a collection of places around the world that have been the focus for deeply odd experiences and supernatural beliefs, locations that have generated fear or wonder, and often both, for centuries. If you have the time and budget (you may need to summon the spirit of a rich relative to tell you where the treasure is buried), you could use it as a travel guide to navigate you through the complex diversity of human belief in the paranormal around the globe, but, for now, just enjoy the fact that each of these 'haunted' places is testament to the fact that we know far less about the way our world works than we like to think we do, and that the hunt to fill in the gaps in our knowledge is bloody good mysterious fun.

Danny Robins

Introduction

At the central heart of all human experience lies belief. Every culture, religion, creed, nationality and language is rooted in its own set of beliefs. These have shaped not only us as human beings but also our architecture, food, fashion, dialects, rituals and psychology. Even to 'not believe' is in, and of itself, a belief. My life as a parapsychologist has been spent fascinated by these customs and practices. Why do the people of Bolivia bury the foetuses of llamas under new buildings? Why is the great Gangkhar Puensum mountain in Bhutan closed to humans? Why do the police clear people from the black-sand beach of Dumas at nightfall? Why do we tell tales of a Hungarian countess bathing in blood? These acts do not occur overnight, nor do they materialize in our cultural consciousness from thin air.

At the smallest end of the scale they are stories and practices passed down through generations. I often think of my late father and I discussing the Broonie (known as a Brownie in English), a Scottish type of hobgoblin that comes out at night, when everyone is in bed, and performs small tasks and chores within the house. In order to keep one you must leave out a small dish with either a bite of food or a splash of milk for it – they are easily offended creatures and if you leave out too big an offering or insult their work they will leave. I used to jokingly refer to my father sometimes as the Broonie; as any time I visited my parents, I would leave my – often muddy – boots at the bottom of the stairs and my father took to cleaning them at some ungodly hour so that when I got up the following morning they were polished like new. They were said to transition to a more malevolent state sometimes and then they were called boggles (boggarts in English). Ones that are connected to marshlands or holes in the ground take on more sinister acts and are said to abduct children. My aunt often told us as kids that we weren't to climb the tree in her garden because that was where Hoggle the Boggle lived. Peering into the tree I could see a brown fuzzy face with two small black eyes peering back out at me. I later learned as a teenager that it was half a coconut that had been nailed high up in the dense tree to feed the birds.

The constant shaping of paranormal beliefs and practices are enacted the world over, every day, without most of us realizing our place in shaping them. Our curiosity in the unknown, unseen, and sometimes untenable, aspects of this existence is what has driven us to survive and persist against unimaginable conflict. Our folk tales, our beliefs, our examination of the inherent strangeness of the world, and above all else our endless desire to understand, is the most important thing we have to leave behind.

Chapter 1

Haunted Places

Charleville Castle

Haunted castle used by secret societies

When you arrive through the gates of Charleville Castle, it's hard not to be spellbound by its sheer magnificence – and eccentricity. The entrance doorway alone is more visually impressive than most you'll encounter, flanked by a tower to each side. The towers, too, have an unusual architecture – they are asymmetrical. The left structure stands tall and narrow, cylindrical, with a secondary tower protruding from the top, and a few windows slitting the stone. The right is shorter, more geometric, with flattened sides and tall windows beneath a crowning top. It connects to a lengthy, decrepit stone building that was once a monastery. The answer to the castle's strange architecture lies in its nod to the game of chess: the left tower represents the Queen on a chess board; the right, the King.

Inside the Queen Tower is the ladies' chambers, containing a red room where doors have been known to lock behind guests, all of their own accord. In the King Tower, you'll find a magnificent library room, built in eight points and following the laws of sacred geometry. Behind a bookcase lies a hidden passageway that once led to the now-abandoned monastery; secret shelves reveal themselves if you know what to pull on, and to reach it you must walk through a hallway where a child of the house once met a terrible fate.

The Gothic-style castle was built by the celebrated Irish architect Francis Johnston and is considered one of his finest works. Begun in 1798, and sited in one of Ireland's last primordial oak woods, Charleville was completed in 1814. The estate itself, however, is much older, dating back to the sixth century. One of the very first monastic settlements in Ireland, the first mansion house was built in 1641 by Thomas Moore. The land passed through several generations before it came to Charles William Bury, the 1st Earl of Charleville, who commissioned the building of the castle as we know it today.

Due to the presiding family's financial circumstances, the castle was never continuously occupied and fell into disrepair over the years; yet, at one point, it held many grand parties, with prestigious guests including one of the great leaders of the English Romantic poetry movement, Lord Byron. The famous English artist William Morris was also brought in to design the extravagant dining room ceiling.

It was during one of these grand parties that death and tragedy befell the house, resulting in its most enduring ghost story. Harriet Bury, the daughter of the 3rd Earl of Charleville

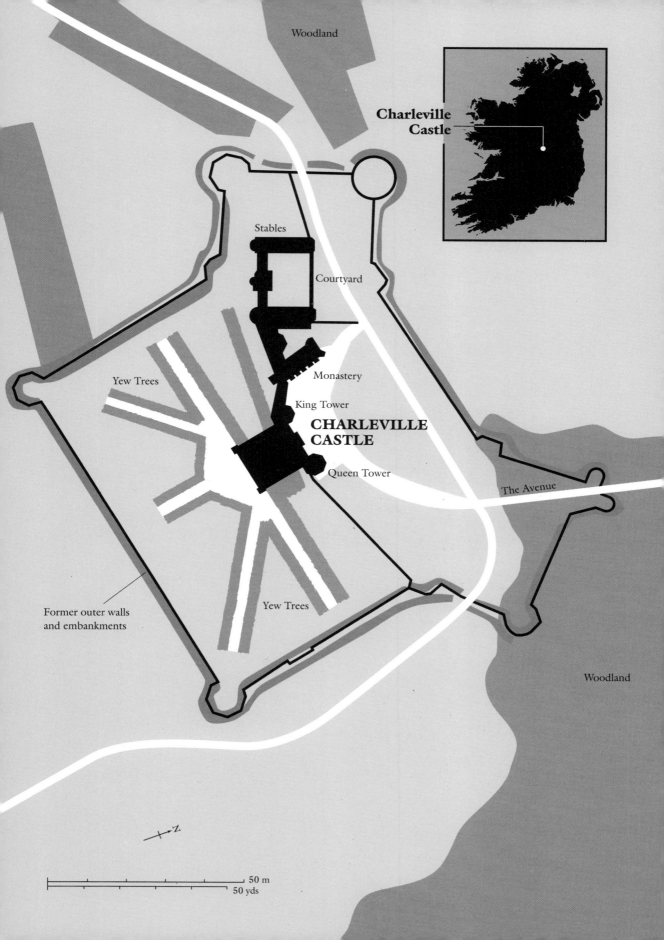

Woodland

Charleville Castle

Stables

Courtyard

Yew Trees

Monastery

King Tower

CHARLEVILLE CASTLE

Queen Tower

The Avenue

Former outer walls
and embankments

Yew Trees

Woodland

N

50 m
50 yds

and just eight years old at the time, was playing on the sprawling spiral staircase of the King Tower. While a party ensued downstairs, and with the governess assigned to watch the children preoccupied, Harriet attempted to slide down the staircase bannister, but along the way she lost her balance and fell onto the stones below. She was scooped up and taken to the library, where she died almost immediately, her neck broken.

Many visitors and residents report seeing a young girl with ribbons in her hair wandering in the tower where she died, seemingly unaware that she is dead. When the current owner's youngest son went missing in the castle, he was found at the bottom of the staircase that Harriet fell from. He reportedly told his mother upon being asked how he got there, 'It's okay, the boy and little girl held my hand.' If we accept that the little girl was ghostly Harriet then who was the little boy? Harriet's uncle died of typhoid when he was just seven years old and many believe the ghost boy to be him.

The two young ghosts seem to be more mischievous than frightening in nature. The conservation manager of the castle was lured down to the dungeon by children's voices not too many years ago, shouting and laughing and playing, clear as day. He followed the voices all the way down into the darkest and furthermost point of the basement only to have the noise suddenly vanish. He lit a match and found nothing there.

And what of the Queen Tower? Here, you will find 'the red room', a chamber built to reflect the sacred geometry and to counter the library of the King Tower. Guests often find themselves locked in this room. After they enter, the door swings shut and locks behind them, which should be impossible, given no keys exist. The children, perhaps, once again playing tricks on guests? The nursery resides at a dizzying height at the very top of the spiral staircase, which begins to twist and warp as you climb it, giving the sensation of being in a carnival fun house. This room has perhaps the most actively reported paranormal activity of all. Many old toys still reside in the room, said to move of their own accord. The daughter of the current owner was once locked in a cupboard in the nursery. Alone, she leaned in to look for something and felt the door slam shut and lock behind her, even though, once again, there was no key in that lock.

This room has strange large shadows that swoop suddenly across the ceiling, such that one might expect a bird or a bat to be flying overhead but visitors say they see nothing there. The shadows move in and out of the nursery to the staircase, often becoming larger and faster, like people running about. Musical toys go off all by themselves, like some unseen force is triggering them, and people report hearing a young girl and boy, possibly Harriet and her friend, playing in the nursery. And they are not the only unexplained presences.

On the grounds of the castle, you will find ancient trees that hold significance in Celtic pagan beliefs and Irish lore. There are many different types of oak tree but Irish oak in particular symbolizes truth, courage and wisdom. Injured soldiers were often laid in the roots and hollow wells at the base of oak trees in the belief that they would be healed – because oak trees and the fluid they produce contain tannins that have beneficial healing properties. Oak trees feature prominently in the tales and spiritual belief systems of druids, who were essentially the upper echelon of Celtic society. The druids were often healers, poets and spiritual leaders, their practices dating back some 25,000 years. The word 'druid'

itself comes from the Celtic word for oak, '*Duir*'. There are many oaks on the estate and the grandest, King Oak, found near the entrance path leading up to the castle. Lore has it that if a branch falls from the tree, a family member will die. In 1963, the tree was badly damaged when lightning struck it and while it survived, the intrepid head of family, Colonel Charles Howard-Bury, expired several days later.

The oak tree isn't the only sacred ancient tree found in the grounds of Charleville Castle. Yew trees are usually found on the grounds of cemeteries in both Ireland and Scotland due to the pagan belief that they trap wandering spirits of the dead and help keep them confined to the burial ground. When British invaders came to Charleville, they planted a grove of yew trees towards the back of the castle for protection, but it is likely that they were unfamiliar with Celtic pagan lore and therefore did not know that in planting such trees they essentially ensured the opposite of their desired effect – now, anyone who died on the grounds would be trapped there, doomed to wander endlessly.

It isn't that surprising to find ancient sacred trees on such grounds as Charleville, given the first building to be established on this site was a monastery in 590 AD, founded by Saint Colman Elo. While the castle's chapel lies abandoned and in ruins, this part of the castle was likely used for different sacred practices at one point. Charles William Bury, its founder, was a devout Freemason. Ireland has the second-most senior Grand Lodge of Freemasons in the world, and is home to the oldest Masonic Lodge in continuous existence.

You will find several Masonic symbols throughout the castle, most notably both towers are built in an octagonal shape as the eight-pointed star is the symbol of the Masons, and a Masonic temple is connected to the chapel. Many have speculated that Bury had the castle built on a convergence of ley lines and that is why paranormal activity is so high here.

Ley lines are a controversial concept in the paranormal world. It is believed that beneath the land certain streams of energy flow and when they converge, there are strange occurrences. Many standing stones, sacred sites and ancient buildings are thought to be built upon these convergences. People attempt to find these ley lines using dowsing rods, which are long, L-shaped, metal rods that are held, one in each hand; when the rods cross, a ley line has been found. The issue with ley lines is that there are so many different maps of them, nobody can agree on the major ones and so they are difficult to verify.

The belief that Charleville is built on these energy lines may stem from the strange phenomena reported regarding the use of dowsing crystals within the castle. The current owner has reported that if one holds a dowsing pendulum within the towers, it will swing violently to the left. A dowsing pendulum is a crystal attached to a chain or string and is held still while questions are asked. If it swings one way, it indicates 'no', the other way, 'yes'. It can also be held over an object and used as planchettes would on Ouija boards. Scientifically speaking, the swinging of the pendulum is hard to verify as being moved by an unknown force – the movement may be due to something called the ideomotor effect. This is when a person unconsciously moves an object despite fully believing they are holding it still. There are many questions raised by the reported paranormal activity at Charleville. Is it that the grounds, dating back more than a thousand years, hold echoes of all its strife and associated death? Do the ancient spiritual rituals that have taken place there for so long have a connection to unseen forces? Perhaps ghosts linger on, trapped by the sacred trees. Or could it be the residual trauma of the sudden deaths of innocent children, like Harriet? And finally, is it built on a convergence point of ley lines, as many believe? Certainly, while there are a lot of theories, all almost impossible to substantiate, one thing is true: when you walk in the grounds of Charleville, you never feel alone.

PREVIOUS: The turrets and towers of Charleville Castle resembling Chess pieces.
LEFT: An old doorbell at the entrance to the castle.
NEXT: Exterior of Charleville Castle in County Offaly.

l'Ossuaire Municipal – the Paris Catacombs

Underground tunnel network beneath Paris that is home to some six million skeletons

When you think of Paris, you may imagine its romantic architecture, its high-fashion beauty, its aristocratic elite, its magnificent writers and artists or its world-class fine dining – but the City of Light hides a darkness unlike any other city. Beneath it you will find miles of tunnels that are the grisly home to more than six million skeletons. These are the Catacombs of Paris, otherwise known as l'Ossuaire Municipal.

By the seventeenth century, Paris was a major hub in Europe, with a thriving population. Its cemeteries, too, started to overflow to the point that corpses lay uncovered above ground. The city's largest and oldest cemetery at the time, the defunct Les Innocents, had become so overcrowded by the eighteenth century that nearby residents were complaining of the constant reek of rotting flesh. This led to King Louis XV banning any further burials within the city. In 1780, the situation took a dramatic turn when heavy rain caused the wall surrounding Les Innocents to collapse, flooding a nearby property with decomposing corpses. Paris could no longer ignore its abundant dead. The solution was to start storing the remains of the dead in the many abandoned tunnels that ran beneath the city. These tunnels were a legacy of the thirteenth century, when limestone – the stone used to build the city to its sprawling glory – had been mined. Once the veins were exhausted, the cave tunnels were often left abandoned.

It took twelve years for officials to finish moving the remains of an estimated six to seven million people, some skeletons dating back 1,200 years, into the catacombs, where the dead were interred up to 1860.

Today you may visit this underground city of the dead. Although the tunnels are approximately 215 miles (346 km) long, the distance between New York City and Boston via car, only a little over one mile of it is open to regular visitors. The public entrance can be found at 1 Avenue du Colonel Henri Rol-Tanguy. After descending a narrow stairwell into darkness and passing along a long, twisting tunnel – the sound of water from the hidden aqueduct serenading them – visitors find themselves in front of a sculpture created before the tunnels became catacombs, of Port-Mahon, by a quarry inspector. An inscription at the portal to the ossuary reads: *'Arrête, c'est ici l'empire de la mort!'*: or, *'Stop! This is the empire of death!'*.

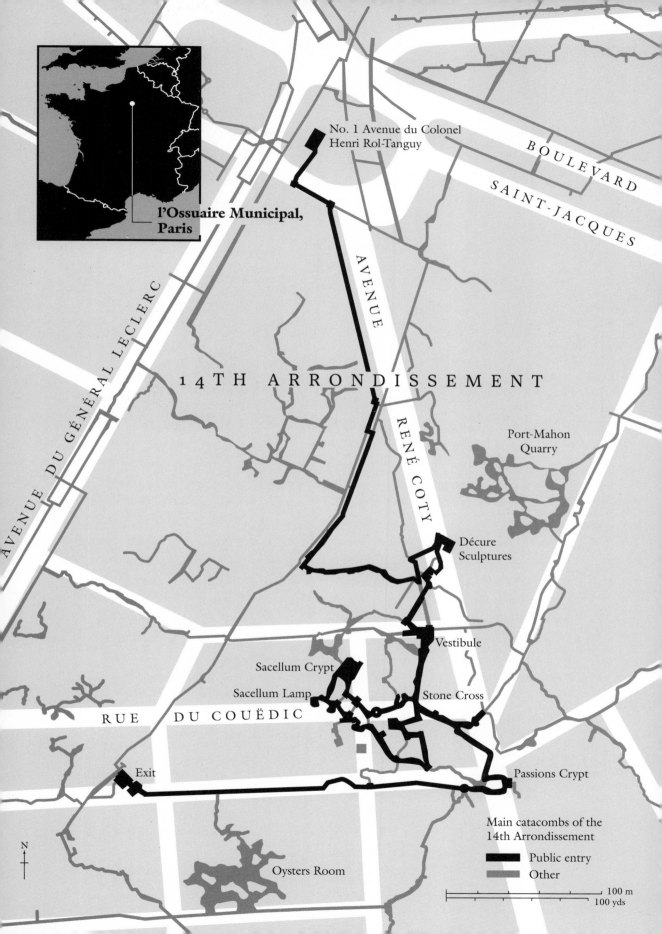

l'Ossuaire Municipal,
Paris

No. 1 Avenue du Colonel
Henri Rol-Tanguy

BOULEVARD

SAINT-JACQUES

AVENUE

RENÉ COTY

AVENUE DU GÉNÉRAL LECLERC

14TH ARRONDISSEMENT

Port-Mahon
Quarry

Décure
Sculptures

Vestibule

Sacellum Crypt

Sacellum Lamp

Stone Cross

RUE DU COUËDIC

Exit

Passions Crypt

Main catacombs of the
14th Arrondissement

Public entry

Other

N

Oysters Room

100 m
100 yds

The catacombs demonstrate the most visually accurate representation of the theosophical concept 'as above, so below'. This is the belief that everything is magnified three-fold throughout the universe and that all things must exist with an equal counter. Above ground, Paris is one of the most desirable and illuminating testaments to so many feats of greatness that it becomes a living ode to what it means to be alive, a beacon of light. Beneath, its architecture is equally beautiful but composed of corpses instead of limestone, the artistry made of skulls: it is a kingdom not of light, but of darkness supreme.

The catacombs are, unsurprisingly, home to many eerie myths and legends, most notably the legend of the found footage that has inspired at least one horror film. In the early 1990s, a group of cataphiles (experts on the catacombs who explore them regularly) came across a video camera lying on the ground. The footage on it showed a man holding the camera who was clearly lost in the vast tunnels of bones and whose mind had utterly unravelled. The video is fairly short and can be found on YouTube with a quick search. It ends with him running manically, as if being chased by something, and eventually dropping the camera into a puddle where it remained. To this day nobody knows who he is or if he lived; certainly, a body was never recovered.

He's not the only man to have become lost and possibly died in the catacombs, however. In 1793, in the midst of the French Revolution, a man named Philibert Aspairt was a security guard at the Val-de-Grâce Hospital. While likely intoxicated, he went into the catacombs via a staircase in the hospital courtyard. Philibert ventured in too far and, armed only with a single candle, became lost and confused; once the candle extinguished, he was left alone in the labyrinth of skeletons and utter darkness. His body was found eleven years

later and he was buried where he was found, sadly, only a few feet from an exit he couldn't see. He is now regarded as the protector of the catacombs and every 3rd of November his ghost is said to rise and haunt the tunnels.

The living have also contributed to its mythology. In 2004, police officers in the restricted tunnels discovered a truly bizarre set-up: a PA system using pirated electricity to blare recordings of barking dogs, surrounded by a bar, living area and cinema for twenty people that had been carved into the stone walls themselves. Even more unsettling was the discovery that the ceiling was wired with cameras watching them. When they returned the following day, the entire set-up had simply vanished, including the phone lines. All that remained was a single note that read: *'Ne cherchez pas'* – *Do not search*. A rather chilling threat.

The paranormality and strangeness of the ossuary may stem from its obvious priming effect on our brains; walking into a gigantic underground cemetery immediately predisposes us to believing that ghosts do dwell there. That aside, its true horror lies in its very real ability to be lethal, as several people have become lost and died trying to escape this labyrinth of corpses – as Philibert and the unnamed camera operator show. Hypothermia and exposure can result in hallucinations and chaotic behaviour, which may explain the recovered video camera footage. The sheer size of the catacombs – they reach almost 200 feet (60m) below sea level – allows for unending mystery as more discoveries are made. There are still large sections that remain uncharted. We have to assume that we do not yet know all of its secrets. But if we believe that the dead are not to be disturbed without consequence, moving hordes of them over many years to create an underground city provides us with an immediate answer to the question of why the catacombs of Paris are haunted.

The Chase Vault

A 200-year-old crypt with moving coffins

Oistins is a picturesque coastal city in the parish of Christ Church, located at the most southern point of the Caribbean island of Barbados. Surrounded by white sandy beaches and sparkling pale blue water, it looks like the sort of idyllic place one expects to find on a postcard. Yet beyond the sunshine and beauty lies a darker tale.

The Christ Church Parish Church in Oistins was built in 1935 but is the fifth church here. Previous incarnations were destroyed by hurricanes, fires or floods. It is not unusual to have a church destroyed and rebuilt, yet by the fifth attempt one begins to wonder if forces unknown have a reason for wanting to prevent a sacred site being erected on this particular location. Does it perhaps have something to do with the nearby Chase Vault?

The mysterious case of The Chase Vault began in 1812, after the death of Colonel Thomas Chase. A wealthy local landowner and enslaver, Chase had a reputation for being so cruel and violent that some slaves threatened to kill him. Chase appears to have died by his own hand, but the suicide was never officially declared, which allowed him to be interred in the family vault, in August 1812. When the vault was opened, however, the onlookers gasped in horror. Originally built in 1724, the vault had been purchased by the Chase family when one of the Colonel's children, Mary Ann Chase, died at just two years of age. The Chase family was plagued by further tragedy when Mary's older teenage sister, Dorcas, died a few years later after starving herself to death. Both were interred within the vault – Mary in a tin coffin, Dorcas in one made of lead – alongside Ms Thomasina Goddard, who had already been buried there in a wooden coffin by the previous owner of the vault. The Colonel himself died just a month after Dorcas.

The vault entrance was a large slab of marble that required several people to open it and when it was removed for the Colonel's interment, the three coffins were found inside in various states of disarray, standing vertically against the walls after appearing to have been thrown around the tiny crypt with some violence. Yet there was no evidence that anyone had tampered with the tomb entrance or broken in. Other vaults in the cemetery were checked and none had been disturbed, helping to rule out that an earthquake or flooding had disrupted the graves internally. All the coffins were returned to their original resting places and Colonel Thomas Chase was laid to rest among them.

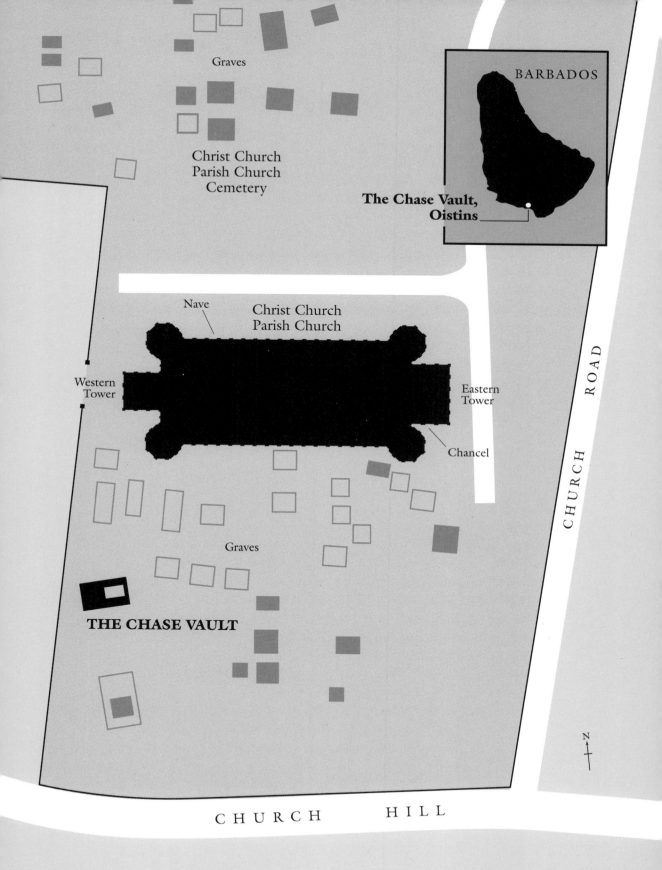

BARBADOS

The Chase Vault,
Oistins

Graves

Christ Church
Parish Church
Cemetery

Nave

Christ Church
Parish Church

Western
Tower

Eastern
Tower

Chancel

Graves

THE CHASE VAULT

CHURCH ROAD

N

CHURCH HILL

OISTINS

25 m
25 yds

It would be easy to dismiss this as a freak accident or bizarre act of nature, something we cannot know the exact cause of but can write off as a singular occurrence – if it weren't for the fact that it happened again. And again. Several years later, in 1816, the vault was reopened to bury two more family members, eleven-month-old Samuel Brewster and his father. Once again, the crypt was found in a state of chaos: all the coffins had moved and the only one still in place, the original wooden coffin of Thomasina Goddard, had been so badly damaged that it was splintering, her skeleton visible.

This time the funeral party decided to set a trap for whoever was seemingly breaking into the vault to disturb their dead. They poured a layer of sand on the floor to pick up the footprints of the intruders. The odd happenings at the vault had now spread throughout town. There were reports of horses being spooked when near the crypt and one woman said she'd passed the vault and heard strange and frightening sounds coming from within. As fear grew, so did curiosity about the vault and its contents. It was reopened. Once again, the coffins had been flung about but the rest of the tomb, the sand included, remained completely untouched. The vault was investigated thoroughly in order to check for secret passageways or doors that may have provided an alternative way in, but nothing was found within.

In 1819, the Governor of Barbados himself oversaw another burial within the vault, this time of Thomasina Clarke, and once the coffins were neatly arranged and the marble door shut and sealed with concrete, he affixed his political seal there. In 1820, just one year after the last opening, the Chase Vault was reopened as strange sounds were heard coming from inside. The political seal was still perfectly intact – as was the concrete sealant around the door, and there were no other signs of tampering or forced entry. Surely this time the vault would be undisturbed?

Unfortunately, not.

This time the men had trouble opening the door, as if something heavy was blocking it from within. When they finally gained entry, they found Colonel Chase's coffin blocking the door. The tomb was once again found to be in chaos with the coffins scattered around, some even on top of one another, some smashed so badly that chunks were missing and the remains hanging out for all to see.

This was the final straw.

Sick of having their dead disturbed and being no closer to a solution or method to prevent it happening again, the family and local authorities decided to remove the coffins and have them all buried separately, elsewhere in the cemetery.

What happened in the tomb? There are two possibilities. One, there were secret tunnels leading to the crypt, which remained undiscovered in the extensive searches. Or two, forces not of this plane of existence were exacting retribution upon a family that had caused so much pain in the local community, and slaves, in particular. Whatever the answer, the now empty Chase Vault remains open to this day.

ABOVE: The Chase Vault where coffins were rumoured to be moved by unseen forces.

RIGHT: Christ Church Parish Church, Oistins, Barbados.

The Borgvattnet Vicarage

Vicarage where ghosts drove out more than fifteen priests

Deep in the forest lands of Jämtland in northern Sweden lies a small sleepy town with an old wooden lodge considered to be the most haunted house in the country. The town of Borgvattnet saw its first inhabitants more than 250 years ago, and one of the first structures built was a church with a vicarage where the priest would reside. The first priest came to live there in 1876, and over several years a total of fifteen priests would pass through its halls, all eventually driven out by paranormal activity, until, finally, no more priests were willing to take their place.

The first tales of supernatural horror emerged in 1927 when vicar Nils Hedlund wrote about them in a letter. Hedlund's mother, Marta, had died in the house in 1907, during childbirth. His father, Per, was utterly distraught. Unable to cope with her death, he elected to bury Marta's body in the garden of the vicarage. When the local people found out, they demanded she be transferred to the cemetery to have a proper burial but by the following day the Hedlund family had disappeared, taking Marta's body with them. Nils later came back to Borgvattnet Vicarage after his father passed away. In the letter he wrote, Nils told of how he witnessed the strangeness of his laundry being pulled deliberately, piece by piece, from where it was drying in the garden, despite there being no wind and nothing or no one near it. This was only the beginning.

In 1930, he was succeeded by a new priest, Rudolf Tängden. Rudolf reported that a woman, clad entirely in grey, suddenly materialized in the room in which he was sitting. She walked slowly towards him and then suddenly turned into a room now known as the Expedition Room, the office where the priests did most of their work at home. Following her into the room, Rudolf found it empty, as if nobody had been there.

The hauntings only became public knowledge after Erik Lindgren took over the vicarage in 1945. At the time it was unheard of for priests to discuss paranormal activity – such phenomena is still taboo in the church to this day, but more so back then. A local journalist had heard the rumours of the hauntings and at a meeting held by the Jämtland County Agricultural Society in the winter of 1947, stepped forward to ask Lindgren about his experiences of living in the vicarage. Not only did Erik publicly acknowledge the hauntings, he documented them thoroughly.

Borgvattnet
Vicarage

R A G U N D A

M U N I C I P A L I T Y
(S W E D E N)

BORGVATTNET
VICARAGE

Borgvattnet

Borgvattnet Church

Borgsjön
Lake

N

250 m
250 yds

Reportedly, one of the most extreme experiences he had while living there was being thrown violently from his rocking chair one night. In his notes, he said that this happened repeatedly and he was never able to remain seated there for long before being thrown to the floor by an unseen force. Erik had experienced strange phenomena from the first day he moved in: he heard furniture being dragged across the floor above him even though he was the only occupant.. This was especially alarming as his furniture had not been delivered yet and all the rooms above him were empty. It was only after Erik went public with such stories that other priests and guests came forward with their own tales of horror and the vicarage became the focus of public attention.

Otto Lindgren and his wife lived there from 1937 and reported hearing footsteps and witnessing the opening and closing of doors by themselves. They would hear someone banging on their front door and open it to find nobody there. Mrs Lindgren heard music blaring in the kitchen and when she opened the door it suddenly stopped, the room found empty; this happened again to Otto when he returned home. Several other priests reported also hearing footsteps in the empty house and garden.

The secretary to the diocese, Inga Flodin, stayed at the vicarage in 1941 and was woken up in the middle of the night, feeling that she was being watched. When she turned on the light, she saw three ladies sitting on the sofa looking back at her. Believing she was dreaming, she pinched herself and wound the alarm clock until it rang. Satisfied that she was completely awake, she studied the three ladies in her room. One was dressed in black, one in purple, the third in grey. All three watched her with sad, mournful expressions. Two sat still

with their hands resting in their laps while the other knitted. Eventually Inga dozed back off; she never spoke of it until many years later.

One of the most tragic stories to befall the house is that of a nineteen-year-old girl who died there, along with her baby. This story has changed over time but the jist of it is that a priest had been having a sexual relationship with a young local girl. When she fell pregnant, she was moved into the vicarage to hide her from public view, so as to preserve the reputation of the church. It has also been reported that she was locked in an enclosure on the grounds of the house. After she gave birth, the baby died – some say she murdered it, some say it was stillborn. The baby was buried in the garden and possibly so is the woman. In the pink room of the house, many report hearing the phantom sounds of a mother and child weeping, and that their clothes are pulled upon and that indentations appear in the made beds as if someone is sitting there.

The Borgvattnet Vicarage still exists today, although it is now a bed & breakfast. So, if you're brave enough to stay in a house that drove more than a dozen holy men from its doors, one where weeping women, poltergeist activity and phantoms are active, you may do so – but at your own peril.

LEFT: Exterior of the vicarage.

ABOVE: The dining room used now as a B&B.

Bhangarh Fort

Indian fort where it is forbidden to stay after nightfall

Nestled into the Aravali mountainside, between Jaipur and Alwar, surrounded by sprawling green in summertime, and moody, low hanging clouds in monsoon season, is a magnificent sixteenth-century fort known to be the most haunted site in India. The sprawling complex was built under the rule of Bhagwant Das for his second son, Madho Singh. Until 1720, the grounds held approximately 9,000 houses. There are five entrances in total to the grounds, with 1.2 miles (2 km) of unpaved road taking you to the main entrance gate. There, you will find ornate Hindu temples considered to be some of the finest examples of Nagara-style architecture, palaces, marketplaces, *nachni ki havelis* (dancers' chambers) and *havelis* (traditional Indian manor houses). The king's palace is located further along, on the sloping hill, with a natural stream that runs into a shady pond. The trees here are more than one hundred years old and gnarled beyond recognition.

There are many rumours as to why the fort was abandoned, chief of them that a *sadhu* (a Hindu holy person) used the grounds to meditate and only permitted the fort to be built there as long as the shadow of it did not reach him or his retreat. Named Guru Balu Nath, he stated that if the shadow fell upon him the fort would fall to ruin. When grand columns were added to the fort, it caused a shadow to fall on the *sadhu*'s sacred space, which many believe activated the curse. The tomb of Guru Nath can be found among the ruins today.

Another legend goes that a holy man practising black magic, sometimes known as a dark saint, fell in love with one of the Bhangarh princesses, Ratnavati. He followed her to a marketplace where he witnessed her buying perfume and swapped the bottle for a love potion. She discovered the deceit and proceeded to toss the bottle into the rocky surroundings, causing a large rock to come loose and fall on the holy man, who was crushed to death. Before the man took his last breath, he cursed the entire village, damning it to desolation. The fort was later sacked by invading Mughal forces, who killed the inhabitants, including the princess.

If you speak to the locals they will tell you more legends, some newer and even stranger, but what can be agreed upon is there are many tragedies that have befallen the fort over the years, including the deaths of several tourists. Three daring travellers decided to stay on the Fort grounds overnight and, despite being equipped with torches, one of them fell into a

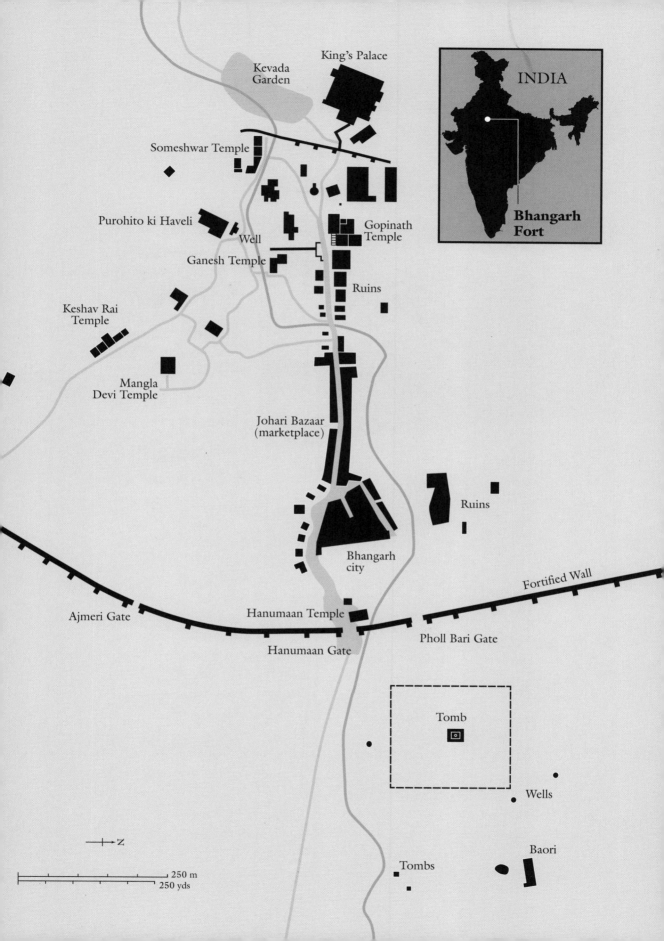

Kevada
Garden

King's Palace

INDIA

Bhangarh
Fort

Someshwar Temple

Purohito ki Haveli

Well

Gopinath
Temple

Ganesh Temple

Ruins

Keshav Rai
Temple

Mangla
Devi Temple

Johari Bazaar
(marketplace)

Ruins

Bhangarh
city

Fortified Wall

Ajmeri Gate

Hanumaan Temple

Pholl Bari Gate

Hanumaan Gate

Tomb

Wells

N

Baori

250 m

Tombs

250 yds

well and was badly injured. After being rescued by his friends, they travelled to a hospital and on the way all three were killed in a fatal road collision. These deaths prompted the Indian archaeological society to put up signs forbidding visitors to be on the grounds of Bhangarh between sunset and sunrise.

The paranormal phenomena reported here varies from visitors feeling constantly paranoid, convinced that someone is following and watching them at all times, to strange perfume that can be traced only to the fort. Other reports include phantom sounds and music, but your ears can play tricks on you in these huge, ancient architectural structures. Then again some of the guards who work there have reported locking up the gates at night, only to hear the voices of their wives calling out to them in the darkness, asking to be let in. This begging is said to continue until dawn. Guards have also heard the voices of their deceased mothers crying and begging for water as they die of thirst. This use of mimic voice phenomena is seen in mythology, with many creatures putting on the voices of loved ones to lure their victims to them; it also makes an appearance in some poltergeist cases. It is perhaps the most unsettling manifestation of paranormal activity.

Another theory is that the threat is not ghostly activity, but rather real – locals looking to scare visitors to the site. There are tales on social media of students travelling from Jaipur to break into the complex at night, and returning to their cars to find locals waiting for them, armed with broken glass and sticks, who try to make them leave with them. Other students,

LEFT: Temple ruins of Bhangarh Fort, the most haunted place in India.
RIGHT: The main entrance to Bhangarh Fort.

who visited at nightfall, reportedly locked themselves in one of the temples, too afraid to venture out. They heard banging on the windows of their car but when they looked outside could see nothing there. Then they heard the voice of one of the guards they had spoken to earlier calling out for help, shouting that something was dragging him away, yet when they investigated, they found him asleep on the floor of one of the temples. They also heard loved ones calling them by their nicknames, asking them to come out, while also experiencing escalating levels of noise. Finally, at sunrise, the gate was unlocked by the opening guards and they were able to run to their car and leave.

It should be noted that many monkeys roam the area, and although they are more curious than aggressive, they have been known to tear seats from motorbikes and steal things. Could the packs of monkeys roving around the fort at night be responsible for the strange noises and feeling that many people experience of being followed? Yet, while this may go some way in accounting for some of the strange events that have occurred there, it does not explain the voices of dead loved ones calling to visitors. That remains a mystery.

Bannockburn House

Haunted manor that hosted Bonnie Prince Charlie

Bannockburn House is a seventeenth-century, Grade A-listed, Scottish mansion house, located just off the M9 road, on the outskirts of Stirling. With a rich history, it is no surprise that the house is the site of paranormal activity.

The house has survived relatively unchanged by time, with the exception of an extension to the rear that was built in the Victorian era on top of an earlier building, Drummond's Hall. Named after Sir Robert Drummond, who was made the Barony of Bannockburn in 1567 by Mary, Queen of Scots, it was built by his grandson. In 1636, the lands of Bannockburn were stripped from Scottish hands by Charles II and given to the Rollo family as a reward for their support of King Charles I during the English Civil War. It is a rare example of architecture from this period and its survival is mostly due to Sir Hugh Paterson purchasing Drummond Hall in 1672, after which he spent several years crafting the building into the Bannockburn House that stands today.

Among the house's many unique features are its main hall, known as the Laigh Hall, and the Blue Room, both of which feature beautifully detailed ceilings designed by John Houlbert and George Dunsterfield, the same architects responsible for the ornate ceilings of Holyrood Palace in Edinburgh, still used by the royal family to this day. Alexander Wilson made further changes to the house, taking out the drawing room floor to give Laigh Hall its impressive double height and adding an extension to the back of the house with a stunning grand staircase.

Despite a fire in the 1970s, however, which destroyed much of the drawing room, the sprawling magnitude of the house is still evident. The house and is environs feature in Scotland's fight for independence so it is, perhaps, unsurprising that so many ghosts feature here. In 1314, arguably the most famous battle in Scottish history took place at nearby Bannockburn between Robert the Bruce and Edward II of England. Bruce's 5,000-strong army defeated the English force of 25,000 (the largest army ever to invade Scotland).

One of the manor's most significant guests was Bonnie Prince Charlie himself. While leading a Jacobite rebellion to reclaim his father's throne and during the multiple sieges at nearby Stirling Castle, he was hosted at Bannockburn House by Sir Hugh Paterson III, using the house as his HQ in 1746. He began a romance with Paterson's niece, Clementine

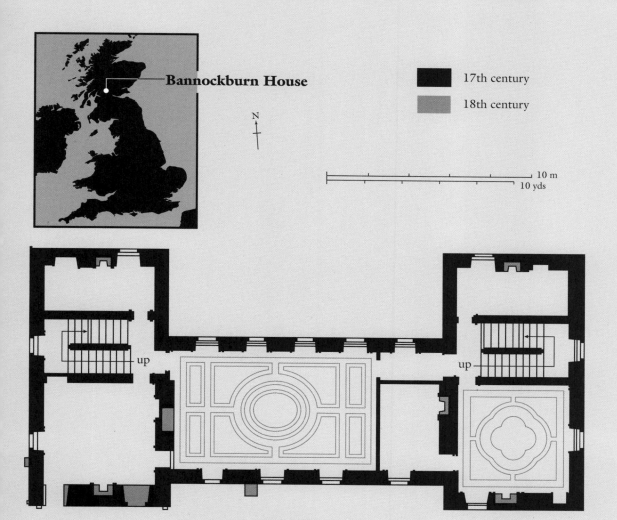

Bannockburn House

17th century
18th century

N

10 m
10 yds

First floor

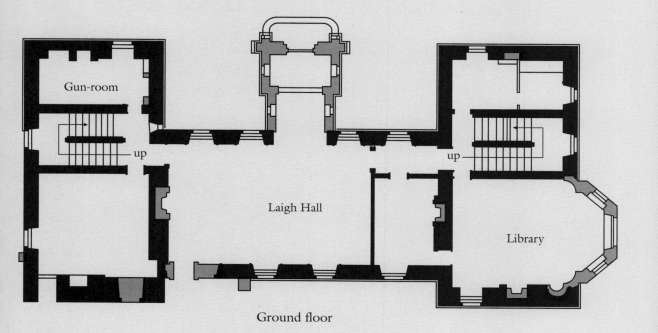

Gun-room

up

Laigh Hall

Library

up

Ground floor

Walkinshaw, who nursed him back to health and became his mistress. She joined the prince in exile after his troops were defeated during the infamous Battle of Culloden in April that year. A young woman is often seen passing through rooms, seemingly oblivious to the living. Possibly Clementine, possibly one of the many maids who worked on the estate through the centuries. She is just one of many ghosts reported to reside at the manor, and is most often seen on the balcony, also the site of a suicide. It is said that Bonnie Prince Charlie himself revisits the room he stayed in where he was nursed back to health by Clementine Walkinshaw. Visitors report hearing footsteps, the scent of strong perfumes, especially rose and violet, followed by banging and then absolute silence and darkness. Ghostly servants have also been seen in the laundry room going about their business, unaware they are dead, but people say that the most chilling area is the basement where something altogether more sinister roams. Paranormal investigators and psychic mediums who have visited the property claim that they have never before encountered evil on a parallel with what reportedly lurks in the lower floors. The issue with this is that 'evil' is entirely subjective – for some, it is simply an intense feeling of ill-will and imminent threat, for others it is extreme fear. Some have attributed the feelings people endure in this section of the house to 'demonic' activity but, often, this is a personification of a feeling that we desire to attribute to a physical form.

On the top floor you'll find a secret room with a doorway halfway up the wall; inside is another room that locks from the outside. The walls are covered with deep scratch marks up to shoulder height. Short of locking giant mad dogs in the room for hours at a time, one can only imagine what went on in there. There have been reports of a loud buzzing in the room, similar to the noise an electrical power box or generator might make, but visitors report that on investigation the room was instead filled with flies. So many that the windows were all but blacked out by them, thousands of them. But at nightfall, the room was silent, the the flies all dead. Their carcasses littering the floor and windowsills like soot from a fire.

In cases of poltergeists, this is often described as a supernatural infestation, one that begins with swarms of insects and scratchings in the walls. A haunting has a similar pattern. Haunted houses can appear as if they are building energy with the activity ramping up in the day-time, long before the chaos of darkness. The flies, in this case, were, thus, perhaps, a warning signal of what might come.

Towards the back of the house lies the drawing room, now charred from the fire that engulfed it more than fifty years ago, and the regal staircase that Wilson added to the house. It is on this staircase that staff reported seeing a man, as real and solid as you or me, descending and entering the drawing room. The man was dressed well and seemed to take no notice of the living watching on in horrified fascination. This appears to be a running theme with the ghosts of the house – that they seem to exist unto only themselves and their own realities, as if played back on a loop, visible to onlookers but not tangibly of our time. From the description, it is likely to be one of the heads of the many families who have resided there, or perhaps even Sir Hugh Paterson himself. Later family ghosts include

LEFT TOP: The bedroom where Bonnie Prince Charlie stayed.
LEFT BOTTOM: Inside Bannockburn House.

members of the Mitchell family who lived in the house in the twentieth century. A volunteer heard the sound of limping footsteps in the upstairs corridor right behind her but when she turned nobody was there. It's believed this was a Mitchell killed in the Second World War, returned home. He is not the only soldier. It is also believed that some of the spirits that roam the estate are those of soldiers killed brutally at the Bloody Fold, a place in a nearby field where soldiers were trapped into a corner and massacred during the Battle of Bannockburn. So many casualties were sustained that bodies piled up and blocked the burn (stream) that ran through the land, turning the waters red with the blood. There have also been reports of gunfire and battle sounds being heard around the property and surrounding areas. But why are some sites more haunted than others? Some believe this is due to what's called Stone Tape Theory. This controversial theory asserts that physical surroundings can somehow record events, and, under certain conditions, these events are replayed – in the same way that music is recorded onto vinyl using grooves, and when a needle is dropped onto it and it is spun at a certain speed, we get the music that was originally recorded. So,

if a brutal murder takes place in a hotel room, that murder is etched somehow into the very walls and fabric of that room, and, under certain conditions, echoes of that moment are replayed, which is why we may see the ghosts of those involved or hear noises of the event much later. The difficulty with this is that in our current understanding of the physical world we cannot ascertain what the 'needle' would be that causes the replay of phenomena.

There are few locations that boast such an array of ghosts and phenomena as Bannockburn House, potential poltergeist infestation mannerisms and a larger and much more sinister presence reported in the basement. Thus, this is not a paranormal location that is simply eerie at night, but one that has a haunting visage even in the daylight. When you walk through the manor's labyrinth of rooms, expect to be followed by more than the sound of your own footsteps.

ABOVE: The ornate ceiling of the Laigh Hall designed by the same architects of Holyrood Palace.
NEXT: Exterior of Bannockburn House near Stirling.

Poveglia Island

A plague island that became a mental asylum

Poveglia Island is seven hectares of land located in the Venice Lagoon, in front of Malamocco, the southern part of the Lido, in northern Italy. It has, over the centuries, served as a military checkpoint and as an institution for the mentally unwell – but it is best known for its use as a plague island.

There are several plague islands in the Venice Lagoon and Poveglia Island was host to more than 160,000 people infected with the bubonic plague. They were held there in quarantine, their bodies burnt or tossed into large dug pits upon death. So many people died here that some say more than half of all the soil on the island itself is composed of human remains and ashes of the dead. This would certainly make the soil nutritionally dense and help to explain the luscious greenery growing all over the island (actually three pieces of land). It would also explain Poveglia's reputation as Italy's most haunted location.

Poveglia has a varied history, dating back thousands of years. Its first mention in physical documents is in the fifth century, when it was used as a safe place during Attila the Hun's invasions during the fall of the Roman Empire. Once a thriving fishing community, inhabitants of the island were forced to flee to Venice at the end of the fourteenth century, during the Chioggia War, and it was then that the government seized the island and turned it into a military outpost by building the octagonal fort that can still be seen today.

When the first bubonic plague, often referred to as 'The Black Death', hit Italy in 1347, it spread quickly and the burial pits built for the dead were soon overflowing, causing further health problems. Colonies were set up to keep the sick away from the healthy in order to curb the spread. People were isolated for forty days to see if they would live or die – this is where the word quarantine actually originates, from the Italian word *quaranta*, meaning forty.

In the early fifteenth century, officials began devising special buildings for the plague victims and built these institutionalized hospitals on the outer islands of Venice, institutions known as *lazarettos*. One was built on Poveglia and they began housing plague victims there in the sixteenth century. People lay dying, three or four to a bed, and workers dragged the corpses out into pits from dawn until dark. So many people were put in the pits that sometimes the living, so ill they could barely speak or move, were tossed in with the

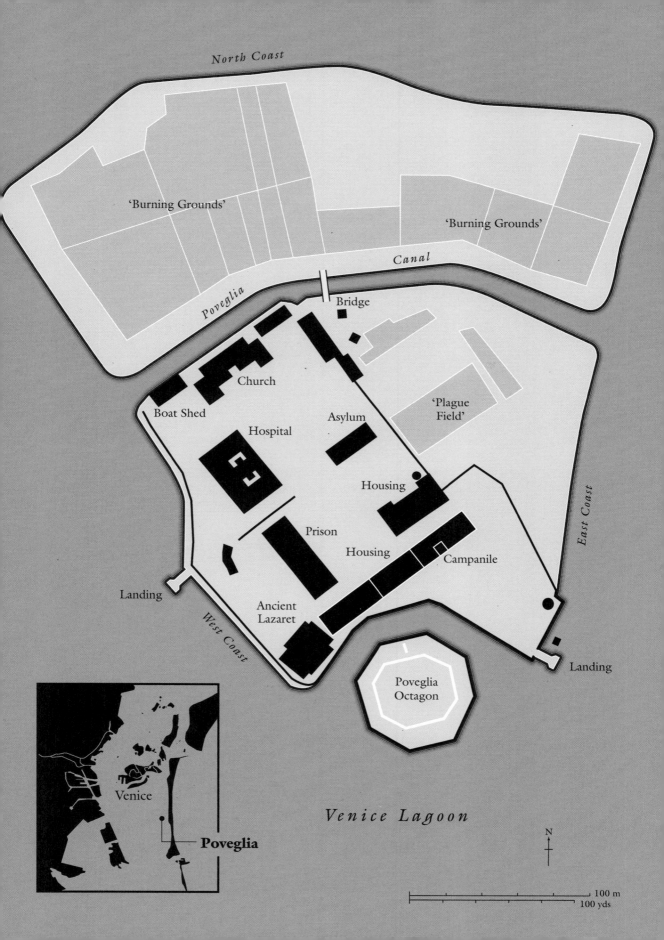

North Coast

'Burning Grounds'

'Burning Grounds'

Canal

Poveglia

Bridge

Church

Boat Shed

Asylum

Hospital

'Plague
Field'

Housing

East Coast

Prison

Housing

Landing

Campanile

West Coast

Ancient
Lazaret

Landing

Poveglia
Octagon

Venice

Poveglia

Venice Lagoon

N

100 m

100 yds

rotting corpses. In the early twentieth century, Poveglia's history became more dark when the hospital was converted into an asylum for the mentally ill. Gruesome stories began to emerge about the behaviour of staff and abuse of patients there. Some said that patients were tortured and experimented on – possibly true given the horrendous level of care and human rights' violations found historically in asylums. It wasn't uncommon for doctors to perform procedures such as lobotomies on patients, whereby a metal rod was hammered through the eye socket into the frontal lobe of the brain, severing connections in the prefrontal cortex. It was thought to treat psychiatric disorders but was largely used to make anyone deemed mentally ill more docile by damaging the brain so badly that they were often rendered into an impaired state, with symptoms including a loss of personality, speech problems, a lack of self-awareness, extreme impulsivity, low intelligence, incontinence, inertia and a loss of empathy. Many patients receiving these types of treatments died and some of those who survived later took their own lives.

The central horror story of the asylum surrounds a doctor who abused his patients particularly cruelly and was driven to suicide, either from guilt or as a means to escape justice for his heinous acts. Another more dramatic telling of the tale says that he was haunted by the spirits of the dead and was eventually pushed to his death from a tower by the vengeful ghost of one of his former patients.

Whatever the truth, in 1968, the building was abandoned, and Poveglia lies uninhabited to this day. Yet several buildings remain standing, including the hospital, with many medical fixtures and apparatus still inside. There is also a church and a boat store. All are crumbling with time and neglect, partially reclaimed by the surrounding greenery, although the bell still apparently tolls in the church. It is this bell tower that some believe is the site of the doctor's grisly death. One story tells of a nurse, said to have witnessed his death, reporting that he didn't die immediately but rather was surrounded by a strange fog that engulfed him, leaving him lifeless, adding to the myths about the paranormal activity on this island.

Despite many attempts to revitalize the island, including one in the 1990s to put a youth hostel there, nothing has taken. At the time of writing, it remains closed to visitors. A few journalists and explorers have been able to gain access and there are a handful of videos online charting the dilapidation and neglect, all of which add to Poveglia's allure as the 'island of ghosts'.

LEFT TOP: Aerial view of the plagued ghost island of Poveglia in Venice.
LEFT BOTTOM: A bed remains in one of the dormitories in the psychiatric ward of the abandoned hospital.

The Winchester Mystery House

Architectural marvel built by heiress of a firearms fortune

Located in San Jose, the Winchester Mystery House is an architectural wonder, developed by Sarah Winchester over several decades. Rumoured to be the location of many paranormal activities, the house has attracted great interest over the years and inspired many a story. In 2018, it was even turned into a film, starring Helen Mirren as Sarah, focusing on her belief in spiritualism and the ghostly activity she believed occurred in the house.

What brought Sarah to the house in California? Tragedy. In 1862, Sarah married William Wirt Winchester, who helped establish the Winchester Repeating Arms company, where he was the company treasurer. The gun company was extremely lucrative, but the family was plagued by misfortune. In 1866, Sarah and William had a daughter who only lived for a month before succumbing to marasmus (severe malnutrition). Later, in a space of just six months, starting in the autumn of 1880 and spanning through to the spring of 1881, Sarah's mother and father-in-law both died, and then her husband died of tuberculosis. Sarah inherited a substantial fortune and after her eldest sister died in 1884, she decided to move to San Jose in California, where she purchased an eight-room farmhouse and embarked on a truly staggering architectural renovation project, which lasted until her death in 1922.

Sarah had a keen interest in architecture and was inspired by the new ideas she witnessed at the World's Fair, a travelling show that displayed the best and brightest ideas from each nation around the world. From 1886, she expanded the house until it became a gargantuan mansion sprawling over 24,000 feet (7,300 m) with 10,000 windows, 160 rooms, 2,000 doors and 47 staircases. Sarah oversaw and designed all the plans herself. She would obsessively begin work, have it stripped down when it failed to meet her expectations and then have the workers begin again immediately. One seven-storey tower was built, knocked down and rebuilt sixteen times. This led the house to take on its legendary labyrinth-like style, with windows to the outside blocked off by interior walls and staircases that fold back on themselves. Spider-web designs on the stained-glass windows cast strange patterns; others hold Shakespearean quotes. There are furnishings from Asia, art from France and chandeliers from Germany. Although Sarah's pioneering design work is admirable, what drove this wealthy, intellectual socialite to obsessively craft such a convoluted house, now listed as an architectural marvel of the world? The answer is where fiction and reality blur. Some believe the tragedy Sarah endured

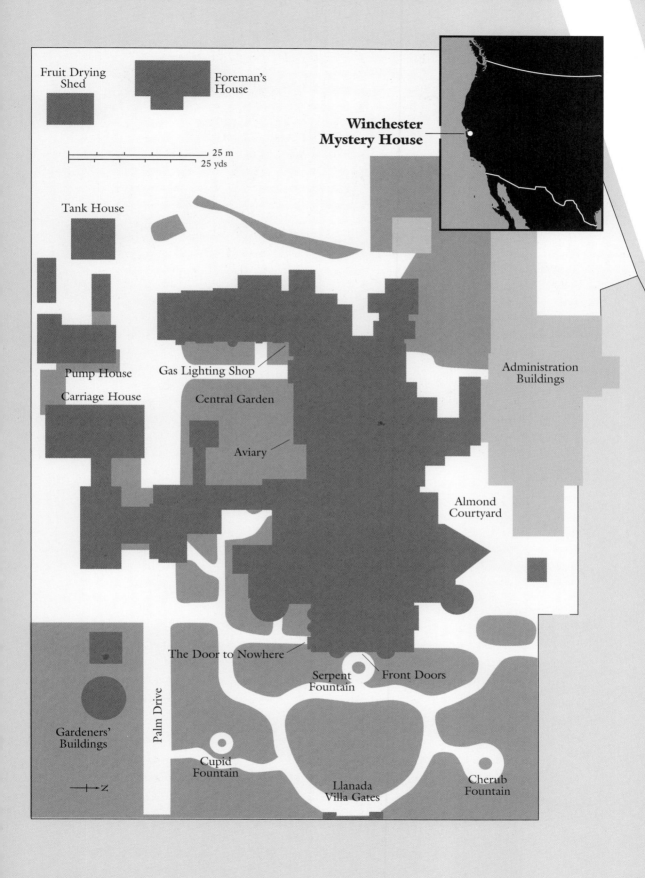

Fruit Drying
Shed

Foreman's
House

**Winchester
Mystery House**

25 m
25 yds

Tank House

Pump House

Gas Lighting Shop

Carriage House

Central Garden

Aviary

Administration
Buildings

Almond
Courtyard

The Door to Nowhere

Serpent
Fountain

Front Doors

Palm Drive

Gardeners'
Buildings

Cupid
Fountain

Llanada
Villa Gates

Cherub
Fountain

→ z

before she moved to California made her turn to spiritualism, a not-uncommon interest in Victorian society. Others argue that the house was built in such a manner as to trap the ghosts of those killed by the guns that Sarah's inherited fortune was built on. Many believe the house has occult elements, notably that it features patterns of the number thirteen. Among other theories are that Sarah believed she would die when construction on the house was halted, so kept on building, and that Sarah's decision to move to California and start the project was based on the advice of a psychic medium. But these theories are widely criticized and in interviews of the time Sarah explained that she built the house in order to create jobs and explore her artistic love of interior and architectural design. Whatever you choose to believe, the house has acquired quite a reputation as a place of paranormal activity.

As her health declined, Sarah became increasingly reclusive and this only deepened the mystery surrounding both her and her house. After her death, the house was sold to John and Mayme Brown, who opened it as a tourist attraction, advertising it on large billboards as a mystery house that implied paranormal elements. Tour guides have been reported to have told ghost stories and implied that Sarah had become obsessed with the paranormal and was deeply superstitious. She was even rumoured to hold séances in the Blue Room to communicate with the dead who plagued her – but records show that room to actually be the gardener's.

Guests have reported strange smells, sudden cold spots, doors and windows slamming of their own accord, phantom footsteps and a constant feeling of being watched. Given the labyrinthine structure, noise may be distributed, and, echo in unusual ways. Similarly,

LEFT: One of many examples of the complex woodwork within the house.
RIGHT: The house has 47 staircases in total, many colliding with one-another.

draught and heat distribution may vary, not to mention that an old house such as this one will 'settle', resulting in disembodied creaking and banging. Given the priming effect of believing they are entering a haunted house, it is likely that guests would be susceptible to confirmation bias – this is when our brains naturally seek information that confirms previously held ideas or notions.

If you have had experiences at the house, they cannot be discounted, but sometimes places become paranormal locations because the living have desired them to be so, either to explain a strangeness they do not understand or because such things create an opportunity for profit. Whether Sarah Winchester's house is a legitimate paranormal location depends on your experiences there.

Chapter 2

Witchcraft

El Mercado de las Brujas

Witches struck by lightning sell supernatural charms here, including llama foetuses

La Paz is built at 13,123 feet (4,000 m) above sea level in a canyon clearing created by the Choqueyapu River, surrounded by snow-capped mountains. A breathtaking place, it was once the site of an Inca city and later became a major trading route established by Spanish conquistadors from the sixteenth century, but before that the Aymarà people, with their rich culture, language and traditions, lived there. Today, you can find some of their goods in El Mercado de la Brujas, a market selling items of a more spiritual, some might say, supernatural variety.

Despite Bolivia adhering strongly to the Spanish Catholic belief system, post-Spanish colonization, much older Indigenous spiritual beliefs are interwoven into life here. After becoming subjects of the Inca Empire and later the Spanish, the Aymarà people had to find a way to mix the new Christian beliefs often enforced on them with that of their underlying ancient customs and traditions, often involving tributes to the spirits to help people on their way. Many of these can be picked up at El Mercado even today.

Protection is perhaps the most common theme of spiritual beliefs in Bolivia – and of many other religions and practices around the world. In the city of Potosí in the southern highlands, legend has it that Lord of the Underworld El Tío (The Uncle) lives in El Cerro Rico (The Rich Hill), the mountain where men mine for silver. The life expectancy of a miner here is only about thirty-five years and so the miners have built shrines to El Tío and adorn them with streamers, cigarettes and coca leaves, hoping to be spared. Similarly, when new buildings are constructed in Bolivia, the dead foetus of a llama is buried under the foundations in order to bless the project and protect the residents. This ritual of committing an innocent life form to the earth is done to appease and give thanks to Pachamama – the 'world mother' from Inca mythology, who is the prominent deity of fertility and, due to a blending with Roman Catholicism, is often seen as syncretic with the figure of the Virgin Mary. And where, if one were so inclined, could you buy a llama foetus to bury underneath your house? At El Mercado de las Brujas, of course.

This 'witchcraft' market is located in the centre of La Paz on the cobbled street of Calle Melchor Jiménez. The marketplace is run by local 'witch doctors' and spiritual healers known as Yatiri. They are a specialist subclass of Quilliri (traditionalist healers among the

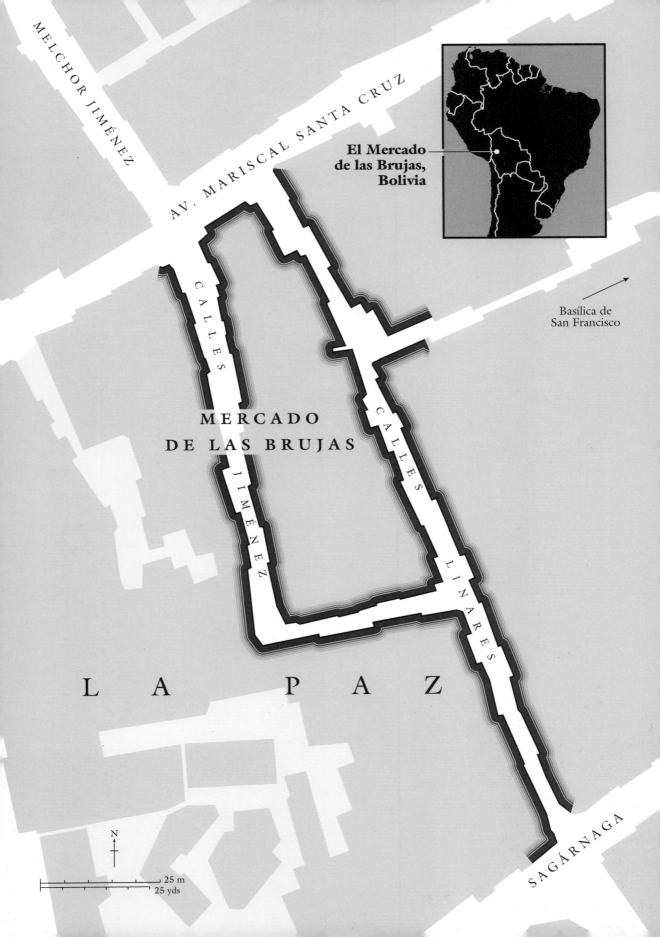

MELCHOR JIMÉNEZ

AV. MARISCAL SANTA CRUZ

El Mercado
de las Brujas,
Bolivia

Basílica de
San Francisco

CALLES

MERCADO
DE LAS BRUJAS

CALLES

JIMÉNEZ

LINARES

L A   P A Z

N

25 m
25 yds

SAGÁRNAGA

Aymarà people) and easily recognised by their tall black hats and talisman pouches worn around the neck. Due to Spanish colonization and the rise of Western ideals, such as individualism, the Yatiri have become increasingly popular as they represent a revolt against Western interference in the lives of Aymarà and Andean people. Despite often being denounced by the Christian Church due to being perceived as a form of Paganism, support for the Yatiri and worship of Pachamama has been openly endorsed by many government officials.

At this market, you can find everything from painted sugar to ward off evil, love potions and coca leaves to stone talismans, dried frogs, hallucinogenic plants and, of course, the dead foetuses of llamas. Understanding what these items are used for is key. The Yatiri may use items such as coca leaves to read your future or medicinal plants to heal your ailment or 'ruwitus', human skulls considered to be of deceased elders, but there are others who use items sold here to enact curses. The Layqa are practitioners, who often live out on the fringes of the mountainside after being shunned by their community, and they use items such as frogs and snakes in rituals to do harm to others – for a price.

Although the market also has a more tourist side to it where you can purchase beautifully intricate fabric goods woven with bright, geometric patterns and small, religious souvenirs for your home, there is a distinction between local craftspeople selling goods and the Yatiri practising magical rituals. Not just anyone can become a Yatiri. In fact, you must be struck by lightning to practise! The Aymarà people believe that the season in which you are born and who your patron saint is dictates what sort of person you may become but confirmation of a calling to become Yatiri involves an unmarried Aymarà person being struck by lightning while out herding the flocks. This makes them *purita* – one who is struck, and they may then go on the path to practise by finding a senior practitioner to train with, a *ch'amakani*.

Many items at the market are used to make a *cha'lla*, which is an offering of reciprocity to Pachamama that takes form in feeding the earth by spilling alcohol or burying coca leaves and placing food in streams. Although these rituals seem fairly commonplace, there are stronger rituals that involve sacrificing a living llama to appease El Tío and there are rumours among guides that larger buildings require a larger sacrifice than just burying a small dead llama foetus under their foundations. The speculation is that homeless men go missing and are fed alcohol until thoroughly intoxicated, then laid in a hole under the building that's lined with the sacred coca leaves and then buried alive; the latter is apparently a necessary part of the ritual to appease Pachamama. But whether this is urban myth is up to your imagination.

Aside from the horror some visitors may experience at seeing dried dead animals and other ceremonial ingredients while visiting this market in Bolivia, El Mercado remains a testament to how the beliefs of the Indigenous Aymarà people have lived, confirming their importance and their place in everyday culture.

LEFT: A stall selling magical totems in the witchcraft market of La Paz, Bolivia.

Siquijor Island

The island of witches and fire

Siquijor is a tiny island province of unspeakable beauty, found in the Central Visayas region of the Philippines. Gifts of nature apart, it is renowned for its mysticism and witchcraft practices. The Spanish, who colonized it, called it Isla del Fuego, the island of fire, because of the eerie glow given off by the thousands of fireflies, which swarm its native molave trees. It is also known as the island of witches and the healing island, a nod to the shamans and *mangkukulam* (local healers) who live and practise there.

The island's origins are mired in myth: the story goes that a great storm and earthquake shook the very seas themselves and in the midst of the thunder and chaos, an island was spat forth from the depths of the seas – Siquijor. Some farmers have since unearthed giant shell casings on their land, supporting the theory that the island may have really come from the seabed.

Siquijor has a chequered past. Colonized by the Spanish, ceded to America as part of the Treaty of Paris and occupied by the Japanese during the Second World War, it finally became independent in 1971. Despite the island's turbulent history, it has managed to maintain a balance of honouring both its ancient, Indigenous spiritual practices and its newer Catholicism, the religion introduced by the Spanish conquistadors.

While witchcraft can be found all over the Philippines, the rituals and terminology used differ from region to region. On Siquijor, the practices – often referred to as 'black magic' in English – are not all to do with healing, as some practitioners work with darker forces and utilize their practices to do harm.

The type of witchcraft found in the Philippines is 'sympathetic magic', relying on 'imitation' and 'correspondence'. Rituals using imitation require human-made objects that resemble the person whose life you want to impact – for example, using a doll – known as a poppet or fetish – that resembles a person you wish to harm. What is done to the figure, sticking it with a pin, for example, happens to the victim. Rituals using correspondence require a naturally occurring object that has a resemblance to what you are seeking to heal or harm – for example, walnuts may be used to treat brain conditions because they are a similar shape, or yellow sap from trees may cure jaundice because they both have the same colour properties.

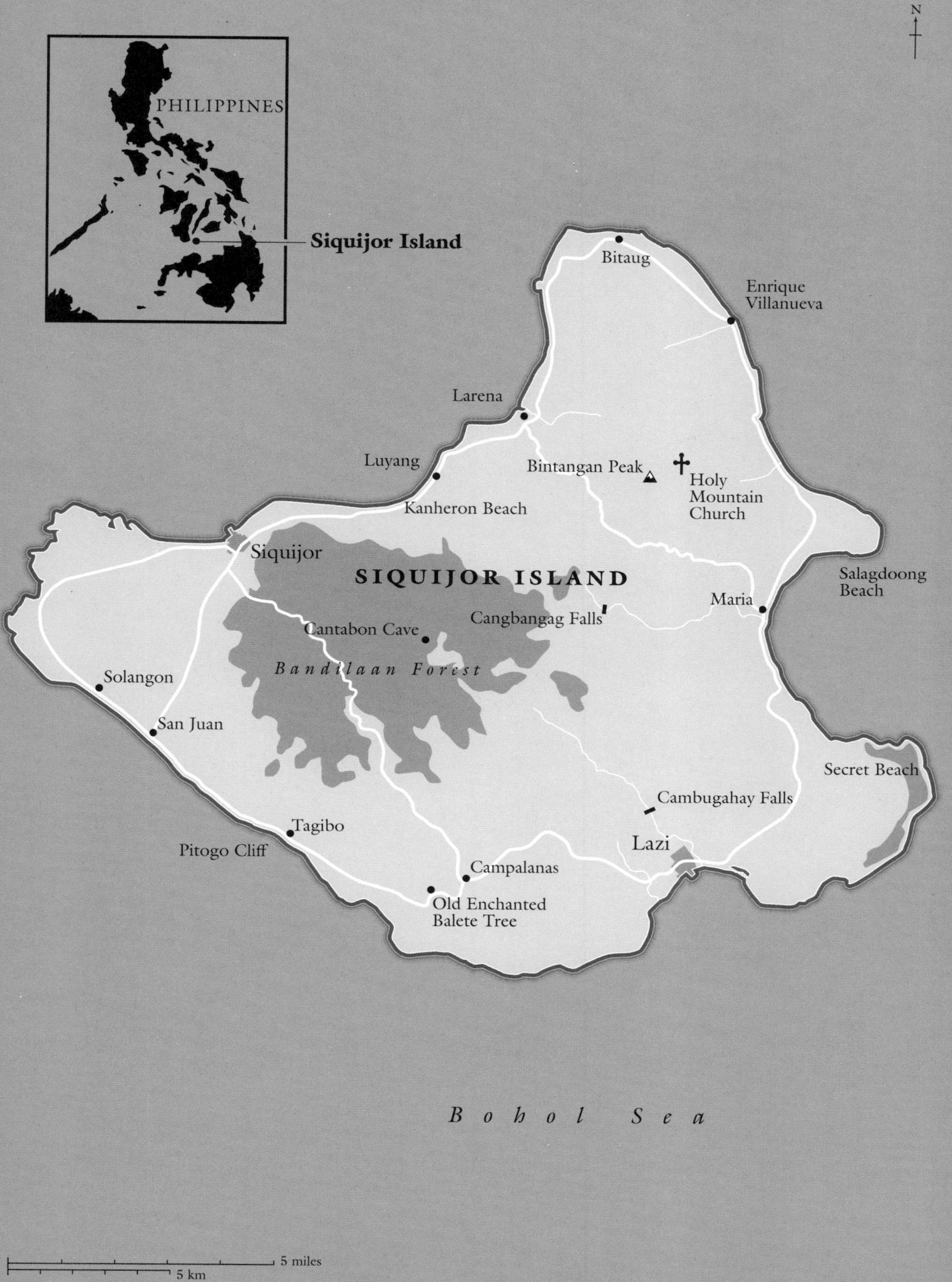

PHILIPPINES

Siquijor Island

N

Bitaug

Enrique
Villanueva

Larena

Luyang

Bintangan Peak ▲ ✝ Holy
Mountain
Church

Kanheron Beach

Siquijor

SIQUIJOR ISLAND

Salagdoong
Beach

Cantabon Cave

Cangbangag Falls

Maria

Bandilaan Forest

Solangon

San Juan

Secret Beach

Cambugahay Falls

Tagibo

Lazi

Pitogo Cliff

Campalanas

Old Enchanted
Balete Tree

B o h o l   S e a

5 miles

5 km

The type of witchcraft practised in the Philippines is usually referred to in Tagalog, one of the local dialects, as *Kulam*. The many varying types of witches, healers, sorcerers and even 'vampires' all have different names depending on where in the Philippines you are and which ethnic group you are talking to. On the mountainside of Siquijor, the *mananambal* use herbs and potions to heal various ailments. This may utilize *hilot*, a traditional rubbing massage, or a 'white magic' practice known as *bolo-bolo*, where a healer is understood to rid the person of evil spirits, by blowing into a glass of water containing a healing stone through a bamboo straw, which they pass over someone's body; as the water becomes murky, it's believed the toxins or dark spirits in the person are being drawn out and they are considered healed once the water becomes clear. A *mambabarang* is a type of witch or sorcerer who specifically uses insects in their rituals and often seeks only to do harm. The widespread belief is that black magic cannot affect an innocent person, so if the spell or ritual works it is because the person it was cast upon is guilty. They will often use a strand of hair from the intended victim and tie it to the worm or bug acting as a magical conduit. They will harm the insect, usually by pricking it with a needle, and the victim will immediately feel the same action being done to them. A more aggressive form of ritual requires a large number of insects, often kept inside a long piece of bamboo and fed ginger root. A prayer-based ritual is held wherein the *mambabarang* instructs the insects to harm the victim and they are then set loose; they enter the victim through an orifice, such as the ear or mouth, and cause an issue relating to that area, for example, a severe earache if they enter through the ear canal. The resulting illness is said to be incurable with regular or modern medicine and the spell only discovered when the victim dies and insects burst forth from the body.

Another, even stranger type of sorcery can be found in the much-feared *aswang*, a shape-shifter that takes various forms, depending on the way in which they may attack a person. They are seemingly supernatural entities that start off as human. As they develop stronger powers of sorcery and shape-shifting, the only way they can maintain these powers is by feeding on blood, flesh and organs. You may find these types of entities are called different names across the Philippines, depending on the form they take, and Western systems tend to use the term *aswang* to simply broadly describe a cluster of vampiric traits that can be seen in multiple mythological beings in Filipino folklore. This may incorrectly include the *manananggal* (a flying torso with fangs and bat wings) or the *sigbin* (a type of weredog/werewolf) but these are actually completely separate entities. Not only do they vary greatly in their phylogeny, but also they are not always directly connected to sorcery. You may also hear the word *ongo* used interchangeably, which is essentially an *aswang*, but it has been created and feeds in a different way that reflects the cultural beliefs of that specific area of the Philippines in which it is being portrayed. How do these creatures come to be? Well, some people believe they are either born to parents who are *aswang*, or they inherit the condition through a type of supernatural transference known as *salab*. This may involve eating food that an *aswang* has put bodily secretions into, or it could be by simply transferring the power via touch on their deathbed. Others still, such as American professor Frank Lynch who wrote about the *aswang* in 1949, believed that they transformed by rubbing magic oil into their skin.

There are some practitioners who do not require insects or effigies to cast spells. Instead they can simply inflict harm or healing with their words; they are known as the *usikan*. The power can supposedly affect not only people but also plants and objects. It is also believed that these people may not even realise they have the power. The superstitious fear of such power has resulted in people being wary of accepting a compliment from a stranger and may lead them to say the phrase '*Pwera Buyag*' immediately after receiving a compliment in order to counteract the supernatural intentions. Unlike other types of sorcerer or witches found in the Philippines the *usikan* do not acquire their powers from others but are rather born with them. Some say that the *usikan* can be identified by their unusually dark tongues and others believe that they are born with a full set of teeth as babies.

As not all who practise witchcraft do so to cause harm, the local traditional healers of Siquijor showcase the positive aspects of their culture proudly during the island's Healing Festival. During this time, many potions and herbs are sold, and the gathering of the ingredients to make them is considered the most sacred aspect of the process. The gathering starts on Maundy Thursday through to Holy Saturday (Catholicism has mixed with traditional beliefs) – the healers believing that there are spirits that wander the island and so a short ritual is believed necessary to forewarn these spirits that someone will be coming

PREVIOUS LEFT: Cambugahay Falls, Siquijor Island, Philippines.

LEFT: Tradional Healers on Siquijor Island brew a mixture of medicinal plants and herbs on the Black Saturday of Holy Week.

BELOW: Herbal treatments and Potions for sale at the annual Healing Festival.

NEXT: Siquijor Island boasts many spectacular waterfalls.

into their land to gather herbs or other items. Most commonly it includes the person saying, '*tabi-tabi po*', which essentially means 'excuse me'.

Of all the items gathered, coconuts are one of the most sacred due to the versatile use of its oil. Harvesting them requires a practitioner to venture to the eastern side of the island and find a tree that bears only one single coconut facing the sun. That must be harvested and carried safely and gently back to the ground. The most sought-after item that many travel to the island for is a love potion known as *gayuma*, which is made just once a year during this sacred healing festival. This is said to be the most dangerous potion by the witches of Siquijor, as if it is used incorrectly, it can result in hatred and anger in not just the one using it, but the person who crafted it.

You'll find that many aspects of the rituals practised here are generational, for instance, the stone used in a *bulo-bulo* ritual is likely to be blessed with rites and prayers and then passed down through either familial relations or from one teacher of the practice to another. Honouring the legacy of that culture and ancestry is key to understanding the life of the island itself.

Rose Hall
Great House

Slave plantation house haunted by legend of voodoo witch

Rose Hall is a distinguished Georgian-style grand manor house located in Montego Bay of Jamaica, and one of the last remaining plantation houses of its kind. Arguably the most famous house in Jamaica, it is hard to miss, with its immaculate rich gardens, boasting panoramic coastal views. However, the 650-acre estate is steeped in a dark history. It was the site of a former slave plantation, where many died in hideous circumstances. According to legend, the spirit of the White Witch, Annie Palmer, haunts Rose Hall. Born in Haiti and a practioner of voodoo, Annie supposedly murdered several husbands and is also believed to have caused the deaths of several slaves through her cruel reign of terror. Visitors claim to see her ghostly form at night on the estate. Rose Hall was divided between sugar cane, and grass and pasture for hundreds of cattle, but it prospered during the slave owning-era, and its grandeur was built on the back of racial violence and injustice. Its history begins with an English colonist named Henry Fanning purchasing 290 acres of land in the parish of St James in 1746, which formed the core of the estate. A year later when Henry died, it was left to his wife, Rosa. At the time the estate was valued at just over £6,000, most of which was the 'value' of the lives of the seventy-two enslaved people working on the estate. Rosa had three more marriages, eventually to John Palmer, who owned the neighbouring Palmyra plantation. Eventually, in 1818, Rose Hall came to be in the hands of Palmer's grand-nephew, John Rose Palmer, who moved from England to Jamaica to take on the massive estate. Shortly after arriving in Jamaica, John Palmer married an eighteen-year-old girl, Annie Mary Patterson, who became the Annie Palmer of lore, later known as 'the White Witch of Rose Hall'. Born to English and Irish parents, Annie moved to Haiti with her family when she was ten years old. She learned Haitian voodoo from the governess who raised her after her parents died of yellow fever. At eighteen, she moved to Jamaica in search of a wealthy husband and married John Palmer. Within months of her marriage, she became bored of John and is thought to have started taking several of the slaves on the Rose Hall plantation as lovers. When John caught her, she was beaten with a riding crop: the next day, her husband was found dead. Many believed that Annie had poisoned him. One account states that she put poison in his coffee and after he succumbed to it, she locked his room and let no one enter, telling staff that he was sick and on bedrest; this supposedly allowed his

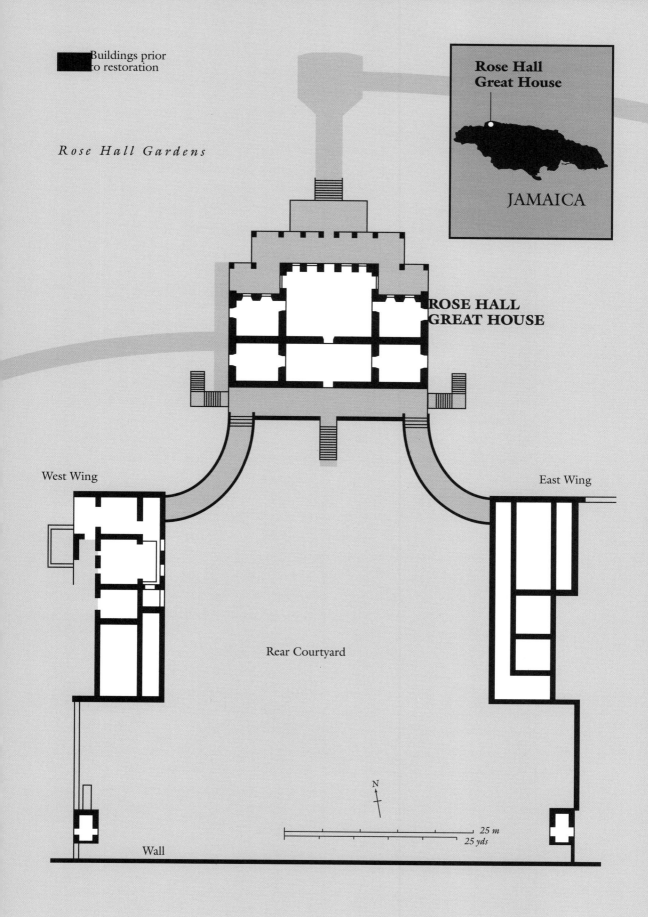

Buildings prior
to restoration

Rose Hall Gardens

Rose Hall
Great House

JAMAICA

**ROSE HALL
GREAT HOUSE**

West Wing

East Wing

Rear Courtyard

N

Wall

25 m
25 yds

body to decay significantly so as to cover any indicators of foul play. The estate came under Annie's control and it is then that her rumoured reign of terror on the slaves truly began.

According to legend, she continued to take them as lovers, when she grew tired of them she would murder them. She also tortured many slaves and was renowned for her brutality, even by the standards of plantation owners at the time. She had traps set up all over the estate so that she could catch anyone who tried to escape. Slaves who worked in the kitchen and within the house were required to whistle at all times when working around food as she believed they stole it and if they were whistling they couldn't possibly have their mouths full. Anyone caught not whistling was rumoured to have been decapitated as punishment for the supposed theft of food and as a deterrent to others.

Annie married several more times and all of her husbands perished. One version of the legend states that Annie killed her second husband by stabbing him repeatedly in the chest and then poured hot oil through his ears to finish him off. This was covered up by the possibly terrified servants in the house and went unchallenged by officials due to Annie's wealth and the local notoriety of Palmer. Her third husband was said to have been strangled to death and this was achieved by Annie with the help of Takoo, one of the slaves she had taken as a lover. When she married her third husband, Robert Rutherford, he took very little physical interest in her and instead pursued the love of Takoo's granddaughter. Annie cast a spell, known as an 'old hinge', on her. The story goes that the spell summons an old ghost and that this would drain the life from the girl, causing her to simply wither away until death. Takoo, apparently enraged at the death of his granddaughter, subsequently strangled Annie Palmer to death.

One account states that her body was left, eyes bulging, on her bed and the slaves later tossed the corpse out of the house unceremoniously before ransacking it in revenge. Another that they buried her body on the estate and burnt all of her personal possessions. A ritual that was enacted at the grave to make sure Annie stayed in the afterlife was performed incorrectly and this is said to have resulted in her ghost haunting the great house of Rose Hall. Hundreds of grand plantation houses were burnt down during the slave rebellion but Rose Hall remained standing. Some believe that the slaves refused to destroy it because they believed that doing so would free Annie from her grave.

While the backbone of most of this story comes from pamphlets published in 1868, which detail the many gruesome tales, they are attributed to Rosa Palmer, the first mistress of Rose Hall. Later, in 1911, a book on the history of St James was published that reattributed the horrors to Annie Palmer. Eighteen years later, Herbert G. de Lisser published *The White Witch of Rose Hall,* a novel that seems to have solidified the legend as we know it today. It is true that Annie Palmer was a real person who lived at Rose Hall, but records show that she was only married once and neither she nor her husband died on the estate. She also never lived in Haiti. So what is the true origin of her tale? Where does historical fact end and fiction begin? Regardless of the truth, reports of ghostly apparitions, whether Annie or her victims, continue.

RIGHT TOP: The Rose Hall Great House, an ex sugarcane plantation now infamous in Jamaican folklore.
RIGHT BOTTOM: The tomb of Annie Palmer, aka the White Witch of Rose Hall.

Catemaco

Mexican city where thousands gather for a festival of witchcraft

The city of Catemaco can be found in the state of Veracruz, Mexico, and draws in tourists for its vast biodiversity and its almost a mile-long (1.5 km) boardwalk along Lake Catemaco, framed by rainforests and Cerro Mono Blanco, the nearby mountain. But aside from being a picturesque Mexican coastal town, its primary attraction is for being the capital city of witchcraft. The witches here are known as *brujos* and are largely male. As with many other prominent places of witchcraft in Mexico, in Catemaco the surviving practices are Indigenous belief systems that have blended over time with elements of Christianity brought over through colonisation, and Vodou practices from West Africa brought over by the slaves the Spanish brought with them.

While Mexico is renowned for its spectacular celebration of the dead, *Día de los muertos*, during which deceased loved ones are honoured with shrines, food, stories, music and a carnival-like atmosphere, it isn't the only supernatural festival in the country. In Catemaco on the first Friday of March, the Congreso Nacional de Brujos de Catemaco takes place, which is the city's internationally recognized festival of witchcraft.

Attracting more than 10,000 visitors a year from all over the world, it was originally organized by Gonzalo Aguirre, who drew many tourists in the 1970s. He famously performed spiritual rituals for everyone from actors to politicians. It is now a fixture of Catemaco and spans three days, where it is overseen by the *brujos* – a brotherhood composed of thirteen of the most senior witches from the area. Of course, over time, many other practitioners of the craft have come forth and many now have calling cards and websites to attract people to the area. However, while there are charlatans who promise to help you and have no actual experience in the craft, generally, those who genuinely practice will often exchange their services for a voluntary donation, rather than a sizeable fee.

The festival opens with a 'black mass', conducted on the edge of Lake Catemaco by the *brujo* mayor, essentially a high priest or high sorcerer of the craft. Certain aspects of the ceremonies are seen as controversial, as some incorporate animal sacrifice and some believe the festival may draw those worshipping *Santa Muerte* (a female personification of death).

One of the rituals these witches practise is known as *limpia espiritual*. Essentially a spiritual cleansing ritual that has its roots in the Indigenous practices it has interwoven

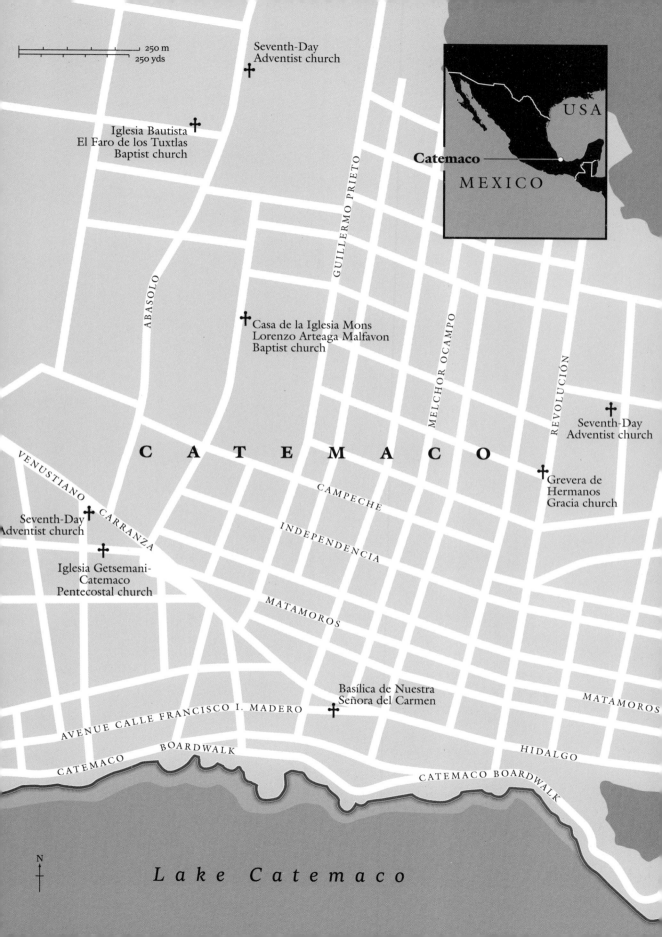

250 m
250 yds

Seventh-Day
Adventist church

Iglesia Bautista
El Faro de los Tuxtlas
Baptist church

GUILLERMO PRIETO

ABASOLO

USA

Catemaco

MEXICO

Casa de la Iglesia Mons
Lorenzo Arteaga Malfavon
Baptist church

MELCHOR OCAMPO

REVOLUCIÓN

Seventh-Day
Adventist church

C A T E M A C O

Grevera de
Hermanos
Gracia church

VENUSTIANO CARRANZA

CAMPECHE

Seventh-Day
Adventist church

INDEPENDENCIA

Iglesia Getsemani-
Catemaco
Pentecostal church

MATAMOROS

MATAMOROS

Basílica de Nuestra
Señora del Carmen

AVENUE CALLE FRANCISCO I. MADERO

HIDALGO

CATEMACO BOARDWALK

CATEMACO BOARDWALK

N

Lake Catemaco

LEFT: Burning effigy at a black mass officiated as part of the annual International Congress of Witches in Catemaco, Mexico.

BELOW: Our Lady of Holy Death, the patron saint of the Santa Muerte religious movement.

prayers to Catholic saints. Sprigs of rosemary are brushed across the body, in particular the head and torso, and then an egg is rubbed across the body in the same manner. This is then cracked into a glass of water and the contents examined. The witch then delivers advice based on their interpretation of what they see in the glass – for example, regarding a troubled relationship or money problems. The ceremony is closed by offering prayers to saints and generously spraying perfume into the room.

Many of the healing-based practitioners are *curanderos*. These are types of holistic medicinal practitioners that are found all over Latin America and some of the ailments they may seek to cure include *susto*, a form of chronic somatic suffering resulting from a traumatic experience, warding off vampiric-type spirits, cancelling out hexes put on a person by a witch, clearing *mal aire* ('evil air'), and treating *mal projimo*, a malady or harm caused to a person by a bad neighbour or others who talk negatively about a person. *Susto*, in particular, is a widespread illness that crops up in Latin and Hispanic cultures, where it is believed that a person can essentially lose their soul due to a traumatic experience.

The *curanderos* may also seek to help people who have encountered *duendes*. They are spirit-like creatures such as pixies, imps, faeries, dwarves and trolls. Encounters with these creatures can be beneficial but at other times may create problems and so the person seeks a healer to clear the effects cast upon them. It is believed that these creatures reside in the forests and countryside, including the rainforest areas of Catemaco. Some believe that they may be guarding the sacred forest and so seek to ward away intruders. There are also rumours of *naguales*, a type of shape-shifting witch who can transform into animals, such as pumas and jaguars, and stalk the forests at night.

Some aspects of the rituals performed here were brought over by Cuban slaves, practising what is known as *Santería*, a diasporic African religion that developed in the nineteenth century. It is a mixture of Yoruba and Roman Catholic beliefs, with a focus on *orishas*, which are forms of deities, making it polytheistic in nature.

In Santería, rituals and practices are more important than faith and believing, it is also centred around a hierarchy where one has to be initiated by ceremony and these sacred ceremonies are often shrouded in secrecy. One of its main rituals is *toque de Santo*, which is a lengthy ritual that lasts for hours and uses special double-headed drums called *batá*. These drums are essentially baptized and are pounded rhythmically in order to draw the deity called *Orisha* to Earth, at which point this deity can possess one of the believers. It is believed that *Orisha* can make someone sick or cause harm and that this supernatural affliction cannot be healed with Western medicine. It is also believed that the spirit of a dead person may attach itself to someone and cause harm, either physically or psychically. The blending of this belief system brought over by the Cubans with the older Indigenous systems that predate Spanish colonization all lend themself to the melting pot of witchcraft that can be found
in Catemaco.

Most witches in the Western world either practise Pagan or Drudic beliefs, as often seen in the Celtic and European nations, or practise a form of Wicca, as seen in North America. Yet witchcraft is a deeply diverse and varied practice that encompasses many types of witches, a blending of hundreds of ethnicities and their accompanied influences on the rites, and it is interpreted through an untold number of forms of worship. At its core, witchcraft is grounded in utilizing nature to affect change; it is rooted in believing that something is greater than us and that we have an active role to play in this system.

Although many witches and sorcerers in Catemaco practise healing rituals, some may take their power from darker arts and seek to create harm. If you attended the festival in 2023, you would have seen Enrique Marthen, a self-proclaimed high sorcerer who conducted a 'black mass' as part of the witchcraft festivities. Located in a small house on the outskirts of town, many visitors flocked to see the senior witch. Dressed in a golden robe and armed with a large staff topped with an animal head, he conducted a distinctly more satanic-style ritual. These types of ritual often begin with an inverted pentagram on the floor adorned with various offerings – usually tequila, with a small goat led into the throng as a sacrifice. The ceremony is declared to be one of indulgence, in opposition to the abstinence that is often preached in Christian ceremonies. The people gathered here typically seek 'unfettered freedom' and often chant 'strength, power, healing' in unison. The throat of the goat is slit with a ceremonial dagger and the blood is collected in a bowl where it can then be used to anoint the crowd of followers when sprayed from the branch of a pepper tree. A large naked statue of Satan appearing as the horned god watches over the ceremony and when the ritual is concluded, Marthen demands that they ask a favour of Satan that year, demand a need that must be met and everyone must exit the room backwards, so as not to turn their back on the demonic figure.

Marthen concluded the rites here by reading prayers from the Satanic 'Bible' and then lit a great inverted pentagram on fire to serve as a hellfire bonfire. In the same way that many Catholic saints are prayed to during healing rituals performed by the *brujos*, and holy effigies feature in the celebrations of *Día de los muertos*, the involvement of Satan by some is another example of the syncretic blending of belief systems here. Lucifer is just as much a part of the Bible as the Virgin Mary, and although the Roman Catholics here view Lucifer as the adversary to their God, the more Satanic witches believe that he represents a free and enlightened path. Such is his popularity that Mexico's first-ever Church of Satan is being built in Catemaco.

NEXT: Dried animal remains, candles, ribbons and other objects feature in the black magic shrines.

Pendle Hill

Area associated with one of the deadliest witch trials in English history

The English witch trials spanned hundreds of years, with the main trials beginning in the 1500s and spanning right the way through to the early 1800s. During this time in England alone, up to 500 people were executed after being accused of practising witchcraft. The law they had seemingly broken came into effect under Elizabeth I's reign, from 1558 through to 1603. Elizabeth was the last of the Tudor line and was principle in establishing the Church of England. She enacted the Act Against Conjurations, Enchantments and Witchcrafts in 1563, the second law against witchcraft. This held that those who: *'use, practise, or exercise any Witchcraft, Enchantment, Charm, or Sorcery, whereby any person shall happen to be killed or destroyed'* would be punished by death themselves. In 1603, Elizabeth I was succeeded by James I (also James VI of Scotland and Mary, Queen of Scots' son, Elizabeth's cousin who she had famously had executed), thus beginning the Jacobean era. James, like Elizabeth, had an intense interest in the Protestant-based theology of witchcraft. He had written a book in 1597 called *Daemonologie*, which was a study on both demons and the way in which they manifest and attack people, necromancy and the historical relationships between varying methods of divination that are found in what was deemed 'black magic'. As James I, he had the work formally reprinted and it remains one of the most iconic and infamous texts on the supernatural to this day. This text also heavily endorsed the act of 'witch hunting', largely influenced by James' role in the 1590 North Berwick Witch trials. A major persecution of witches in Scotland, it saw many people from around East Lothian accused of witchcraft in the St Andrews Auld Kirk, a church on the harbourfront of the coastal town of North Berwick on Halloween night. The trial spanned two years, with more than one hundred suspected witches arrested, and it included royal houses and monarchies being dragged into the proceedings. The case was truly sensational and kickstarted what would become a reign of witch fever under James I.

It began with a storm.

James planned to marry fourteen-year-old Anne of Denmark and on her journey over from Copenhagen to the UK, her ship was forced to shelter in Norway due to storms. James sailed over to retrieve his future child bride and the destruction to the boats and horrendous weather was blamed on the wife of an official back in Copenhagen. She was disgruntled by

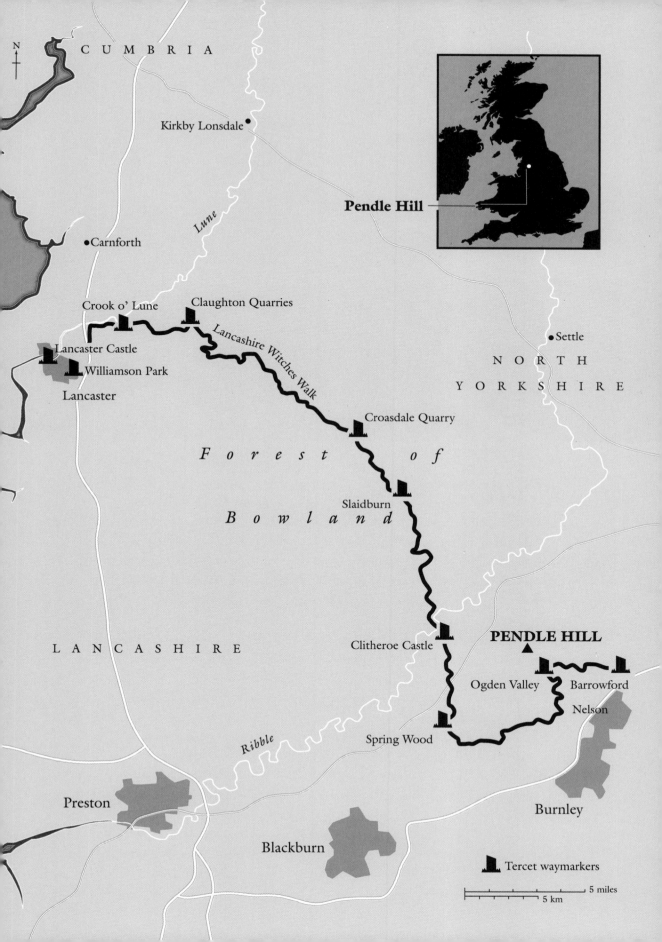

N

C U M B R I A

Kirkby Lonsdale

Lune

Carnforth

Crook o' Lune

Claughton Quarries

Lancaster Castle

Williamson Park

Lancaster

Lancashire Witches Walk

Settle

N O R T H

Y O R K S H I R E

Croasdale Quarry

F o r e s t   o f

B o w l a n d

Slaidburn

L A N C A S H I R E

Clitheroe Castle

PENDLE HILL

Ogden Valley

Barrowford

Nelson

Ribble

Spring Wood

Preston

Burnley

Blackburn

Tercet waymarkers

5 miles

5 km

Pendle Hill

one of the political figures on the boat. Under duress, she gave up the names of five other women who were also made to confess to summoning storms to stop the journey and summoning devils to climb onto the ship. James set up his own investigation on the Scottish side, resulting in the Berwick Witch Trials, where he personally oversaw the torture of those accused. It most famously included the torture of Agnes Sampson, who was taken to the Palace of Holyrood, stripped naked, shaven bald, her head bound tightly in rope, crushing her skull until she confessed. Her naked and deformed ghost is still said to haunt Holyrood to this day.

The witch hunts raged onwards and at the start of 1612, an order was passed down to all justices of the peace (volunteers who oversaw law and order in their country) in Lancashire that they should set about making a list of all local people who did not attend the church services and refused to take Communion; at the time, failure to do so was illegal. The justice of the peace for Pendle was a man named Roger Nowell. It was during this time of compiling a list of religious non-conformists that a complaint was brought forward to Nowell by a transient pedlar who claimed to have been harmed by an act of witchcraft. It was this complaint that would lead to one of the most infamous witch trials in British history – the Pendle Witch Trial, featuring twelve accused villagers from the area surrounding Pendle Hill.

On 21 March 1612, the pedlar, John Law, met Alizon Device while travelling to Trawden Forest. Device asked him for some pins, which would seem fairly innocuous if it weren't for the fact that metal pins at that time were handmade and very expensive. Pins often feature

LEFT: Footpath signs indicate the witches walk with Pendle Hill rising behind.
RIGHT: Statue of Alice Nutter, one of the group of people tried for murder after being accused of using witchcraft 400 years ago.
NEXT LEFT: Classical folk depiction of witches riding a besom.
NEXT RIGHT: (Engraving) Depiction of the young witch Jennet urging her familiar, the cat Tib, to attack her victim.
PAGE 84-85: Pendle Hill in Lancashire, England

prominently in various kinds of witchcraft, but in Pagan witchcraft, which would have been the most common type practised at that time and in that area, they were commonly used in healing rituals and some love spells. Law refused to give her the pins. Alizon claimed she meant to buy them, the son of Law claimed she was penniless and begging for them. Law then walked away from Alizon and after a few steps stumbled and fell down, unable to speak; this could have been for any number of reasons, including a stroke or blood pressure issues. He recovered and managed to get himself to a nearby inn, where at the time he made no accusations towards Alizon. It was Law's son, Abraham, who several days later fetched Alizon and brought her to the pedlar, where she then reportedly confessed to having bewitched him into becoming lame and begged for forgiveness.

Alizon, her brother James and her mother Elizabeth were summoned to appear before Nowell, wherein Alizon Device confessed to selling her soul to the devil and cursing John Law. It was stated that the devil appeared in the form of a dark dog with 'fiery' eyes that offered to maim Law as revenge for him calling Alizon a thief. The devil appearing as a large brown or black dog is common in folklore, especially in England. Out on the moors and in the remote countryside, people often reported seeing a massive dark dog, the size of a horse, sometimes with glowing eyes, believed to be a hound of hell. In folklore, they are interpreted as being messengers of hell, omens of death, phantom creatures sent to drag souls to hell and sometimes they are a form of the devil himself. You will often see them referred to as a 'Black Shuck'; this is derived from the old English word *scucca*, meaning devil or fiend. Accounts of this creature date back to 1127 and they are mostly reported in

East Anglia, in east England. In a 1901 account by W. A. Dutt he described it as having a singular glowing eye in the centre of its head, similar to that of a Cyclops. Jennet Device, the sister of Alizon, claimed that the large dark dog was in fact a witch's familiar that belonged to her grandmother. A witch's familiar is a supernatural entity that takes the form of a companion animal and assists a witch in their practise of the craft. Although the most popular witch's familiars include black cats and owls, a dark dog is not uncommon.

Alizon's grandmother, Demdike, was a well-known practising witch in the area and had been so for decades. She was a healer and *wortcunner* (a person with advanced knowledge of herbs and plants for mostly medicinal use) and was widely accepted, as were many others throughout rural England, as practising her craft. Women in rural areas often had to take on the roles of being midwife, doctor, holistic specialist, herbologist and wise council. Most of those who were sentenced for witchcraft wouldn't have considered themselves witches – many were just women accused of preposterous things and others were simply local healers. Demdike's family weren't the only local family known for witchcraft – the Chattox family, with whom they feuded over stolen goods, were also known. When Alizon was questioned about the Chattoxes, she gave a statement claiming that Anne, the matriarch of the family, had killed four men through means of witchcraft and had even killed her own father, John Device. She claimed that her father had been so afraid of the Chattox family that he had paid them eight pounds of oatmeal each year not to bring his family to harm, and that on his deathbed he claimed that his terminal illness was revenge for not paying them that year.

Both family matriarchal heads, Demdike and Anne Chattox, who were in their eighties and mostly blind, were summoned to appear before a tribunal and both gave open confessions that they were indeed witches. The following statements were, however, likely made under duress, as it is one thing to be practising herbal magic, and another entirely different thing to be in league with 'the devil'. Demdike said she sold her soul to the devil many decades before and Chattox claimed to have also sold her soul to something that looked 'like a Christian man' who in return would grant her desires and allow her to enact revenge on whomever she saw fit. Four of the family members were sent to prison to await trial, and it would have ended there, but Elizabeth Device decided to host a dinner at her family's home (Malkin Tower) where the rest of the family and sympathetic friends attended. James stole a neighbour's sheep for the feast, which resulted in an investigation. When Nowell caught wind of this he investigated the feast and charged eight more people with acts of witchcraft, sending them to prison to join the other four accused.

The Pendle Witches stood trial as part of a larger group of people accused across Lancashire. This group included Margaret Pearson, AKA the Padiham Witch, on trial for witchcraft for a third time, the Samlesbury Witches, whose charges included cannibalism and the murder of a child, and Isobel Robey, who, like the Pendle Witches, was accused of *maleficium* – the act of using witchcraft to harm another person.

The first of the Pendle Witches to be tried was Jennet Preston, accused of murdering a local landowner by supernatural means. Jennet lived in Yorkshire at the time and so was tried there separately at the York Assizes, with the remaining accused tried at the Lancaster Assizes a few weeks later. The evidence against her was that she had been taken to see the body of the dead landowner and that after she touched him fresh blood ran from the corpse. James Device said that she attended the feast at Malkin Tower to seek help with what she had done. She was put to death by hanging.

The trial at the Lancaster Assizes took place over two days and the main witness for the prosecution was Jennet Device, who at the time was just nine years old. The use of such a young child's testimony would not normally have been permitted in court but in James I's treatise on the supernatural, *Daemonologie*, he had stated that the normal rules of trial should be suspended when trying witches. The child accused her own mother of being a witch, claiming she spoke often to the large dog that was the family familiar and asked it to help her cast death upon various victims. James Device was accused of the same crime. Attendees at the feast were accused of plotting the supernatural murders of many people, some by means of making clay dolls of local people who were now deceased, and all but one of them was retroactively charged with their deaths. Alizon, with whom all of this began, faced her accuser in court and genuinely believed in her powers; she confessed openly to *maleficium* and wept for forgiveness. Demdike died while awaiting trial.

Of the all the Pendle Witches who stood accused, nine were found guilty and sentenced to execution. They were hanged at Gallows Hill in Lancaster on 20 August 1612.

Chapter 3

Sacred Sites

La Recoleta Cemetery

Exquisite architectural city of the dead

Perhaps it's not surprising that a cemetery should be included in a book about the paranormal, and this iconic Argentinian cemetery happens to be one of the most beautiful burial grounds in the world. Designed by Próspero Catelin and remodelled in 1881, its 14 acres are a veritable explosion of Victorian neoclassicalism. It contains 4,691 above-ground vaults, more than 6,000 graves and has almost one hundred tombs designated as National Historical Monuments. Its striking white marble architecture features many depictions of full-size angels, draped women, generals, thrones, Greek temples and complex religious scenes. Leading sculptors have work here, their styles ranging from Baroque, Art Deco and Art Nouveau to Gothic Revival.

As Buenos Aires' first official public burial place, the city now wraps around it, and it features quite the list of famous people at rest here – including former presidents, actors, poets, Nobel Prize winners, writers and scientists. All of the mausoleums are built above-ground as the earth has a marshy texture and so any bodies or coffins buried there would most likely be pushed back up to the surface – a grim thought.

The stories behind some of the ornate tombs here and the deaths that resulted in them range from strange and tragic to horrifying. Perhaps the most visited resting place is that of Eva 'Evita' Perón, the iconic but controversial First Lady of Argentina. Despite it being one of the most minimalist tombs, many come to pay their respects here; it was even visited by actor Liza Minnelli. Evita's death is shrouded in conspiracy; although she died in 1952, it took twenty years for officials to release her body to be interred at the cemetery. Originally embalmed, Evita's body was meant to go in a monument bigger than the Statue of Liberty, but when her husband, the president, was deposed in a military uprising, the junta found themselves stuck with her body. Unable to bury her for fear that the site would become a place of pilgrimage, the new government arranged for her to be buried in a false grave in Italy; she was only exhumed and brought back to Argentina decades later. Eva is said to be, exceptionally, buried 16 feet (5 m) underground in a tomb that is 'fortified like a nuclear bunker'. She is referred to as 'the walking corpse' of La Recoleta, as it is speculated the tomb is strengthened not to keep people out, but rather to keep Evita in.

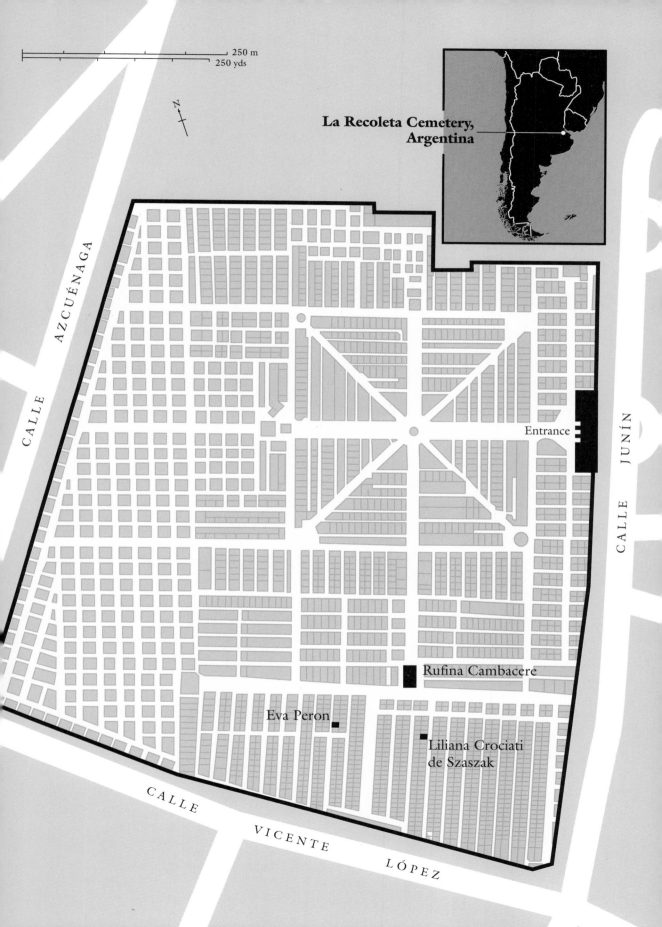

250 m
250 yds

N

La Recoleta Cemetery, Argentina

CALLE AZCUÉNAGA

CALLE JUNÍN

Entrance

Rufina Cambacere

Eva Peron

Liliana Crociati
de Szaszak

CALLE

VICENTE

LÓPEZ

The cemetery is full of ghosts, David Alleno among them. A caretaker and gravedigger here for more than thirty years, Alleno hoped to be buried in the cemetery one day alongside the many notables from Argentina's history. He saved up for years for his own plot and even commissioned a statue of himself to accompany it. As soon as it was complete, he went home and committed suicide. This morbid tale has resulted in many believing that his ghost lingers on and haunts the grounds. Visitors have reported hearing the jingling of his keys as he walks around.

One of the most iconic tombs here is that of Rufina Cambacérès, a stunning Art Nouveau piece depicting a young woman in draped clothing with her hand upon a striking black door beneath gigantic white marble flowers. The tomb is more elaborate than it was initially intended to be due to a shocking turn of events, wherein the storing of her body before this may have been what actually caused her death. Rufina was originally found lifeless and was pronounced dead from a suspected cardiac arrest. She died at just nineteen years old and was to be buried here in the early 1900s. Her coffin was interred at La Recoleta, in a tomb less ornate than this one, likely a family plot. Within a few days, cemetery workers reported seeing that the coffin had moved and the lid appeared damaged. They reported it to her parents, fearing graverobbers had tampered with it. When the coffin was opened, they found Rufina bloody and bruised with scratch marks on the inside of her coffin lid – she had been buried alive. Now having technically died twice, it was assessed that she had developed a rare medical condition that had caused her to fall into a temporary coma-like state, and that she had still been alive when placed into the coffin, after being wrongly pronounced dead

LEFT: The tomb of Rufina Cambaceres at the La Recoleta Cemetery.

RIGHT: The famous tomb of Liliana Crociati de Szaszak pictured with her beloved dog.

by her doctors. Once she regained consciousness, she had then died of exhaustion and lack of oxygen trying to get out of her coffin. The new tomb was commissioned by her mother and the marble feature of her walking out the door represents her overcoming her cause of death. People have reported hearing cries for help and howling coming from her tomb, believing that her restless spirit is still reliving her terrible final moments.

One of the most standout burial plots here is actually a relatively modern one, that of twenty-six-year-old Liliana Crociati de Szaszak. Liliana was tragically killed in the 1970s, while on honeymoon in Austria, when an avalanche struck the hotel she was staying at and killed both her and her new husband. Her grave was commissioned by her parents, Italians who had immigrated to Argentina, and is made entirely of wood and glass, built in a modern Gothic style. The inside of the tomb is an exact replica of Liliana's childhood bedroom. Outside the tomb, there is a poem carved in Italian that her griefstricken father had penned for her and a statue of her in her wedding dress, accompanied by a smaller statue of her beloved pet dog, Sabú. There's a story that the dog actually died at the same time the young lady did, despite being separated by hundreds of miles.

This city of the dead is a reflection of both Argentina's broader love of architectural beauty and its great affinity for life after death; it has become an art gallery of ghosts.

The Hanging Coffins of Sagada

Gravity-defying graveyard suspended in the mountains

For more than 2,000 years the Igorot people of Sagada on the island of Luzon in the northern Philippines have been hanging their dead on mountainsides, rather than burying them in the earth, so that they can be closer to their ancestral spirits. The elderly carve their own coffins and paint their names on the sides. The coffins are hung on the side of the mountains, with metal beams and poles driven into the rock-face and then twisted upwards at the ends to create a form of cradle that the coffin can be placed on.

Older coffins are about 3 feet (1 m) – today they are usually about twice that – the bodies' bones often broken so as to get them into a foetal position, knees drawn to the chin, as it was believed beneficial to leave this world in the same way the person entered into it. Before this, the corpse is tied, with vines and ropes, to a type of wooden chair known as a 'death chair', and covered with a blanket. It is placed facing the door and preserved for several days, using smoke, in order to allow relatives to pay their final respects. The body, in its foetal position, is then wrapped in rattan leaves and placed inside the coffin, wrapped again in a blanket. As mourners gather, the coffin is suspended, and blood or body fluids may leak from the box; it is believed the first person to have a drop of this fluid or blood fall upon them is blessed with luck. In time, coffins may deteriorate and fall to pieces from their hanging places, but many have lasted centuries – although it is advisable not to walk under them and instead to admire from afar.

Funeral rituals that precede the final resting of the dead may vary. Some people have mourners and family of the dead chant dirges and songs for up to ten days, and a pig is slaughtered as an offering during each day of the vigil. Five days after the coffin is placed at rest, the mourners make a pilgrimage to a river where they sacrifice a chicken while offering a prayer to their dead. Others conduct a dirge sung by three men (known as a *baya-o*), followed by an elegy (*menbaya-o*) and two animal offerings; two pigs and three chickens (*sangbo* ritual) and a single pig (*sedey* ritual). The rites are then closed with a song for the dead known as a *dedeg*. Once complete the sons and grandsons carry the deceased to their final resting place. Although there are ongoing problems with the preservation of the coffins, including graverobbing, they are still accessible to those who wish to visit.

NEXT Hanging Coffins on the mountainside of Sagada, Philippines.

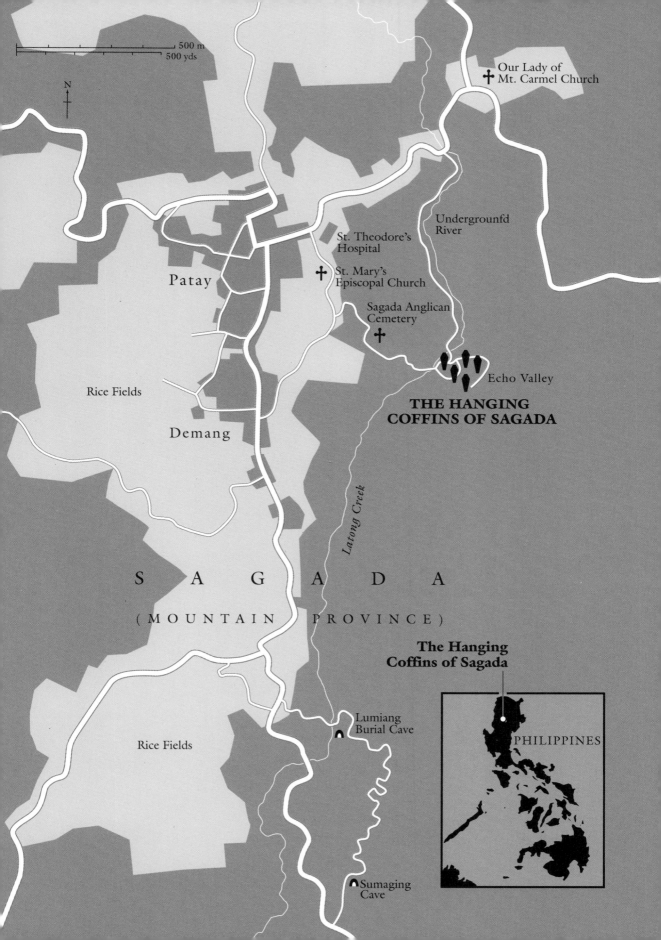

500 m
500 yds

N

Our Lady of
Mt. Carmel Church

St. Theodore's
Hospital

Undergrounfd
River

St. Mary's
Episcopal Church

Patay

Sagada Anglican
Cemetery

Echo Valley

**THE HANGING
COFFINS OF SAGADA**

Demang

Rice Fields

Latong Creek

S A G A D A

(M O U N T A I N   P R O V I N C E)

**The Hanging
Coffins of Sagada**

Lumiang
Burial Cave

Rice Fields

PHILIPPINES

Sumaging
Cave

Borobudur Temple

World's largest Buddhist temple, which was inexplicably abandoned

Built in the ninth century, Borobudur, in central Java, sits on a hill surrounded by active volcanoes. It is the largest Buddhist temple in the world, featuring hundreds of sculptures and thousands of embossed panels that reflect a blend of traditional native Indonesian beliefs and Buddhist concepts. It is built in three tiers, consisting of: a pyramid base with five concentric square terraces, a cone with three circular platforms and a huge stupa. There are seventy-two open-relief stupas on the circular platforms, each with a statue of Buddha. It lay abandoned and forgotten for many centuries, buried under volcanic ash and vegetation, until it was 'discovered' by the British lieutenant-governor Thomas Stamford Raffles, in 1814. Excavation work began in the twentieth century. Many myths grew around the site over the centuries it was lost, and why such a great place of pilgrimage was not just abandoned but forgotten for so long remains a mystery.

Today, the temple is again a site of pilgrimage for many Buddhists and the ascent from the base to the top, roughly 3 miles (5 km), takes the pilgrim clockwise through three concepts of Buddhist cosmology – the world of desire, the world of forms and the world of the formless. Its overall design is that of a three-dimensional mandala, seen to be a map of the cosmos in Buddhist teachings. The sacred geometry of pattern repetition that is found in the architecture here reflects the constant cycle of life, death and rebirth. There are no known records of the construction of the temple, or what its primary use was for, beyond obvious worship, but it is estimated to have taken 75 years to construct and still remains the largest architectural attraction in Indonesia. But why was it abandoned? We know that the capital of the kingdom was shifted to East Java around the same time as the volcanic eruption in 1000CE by King Mpu Sindok, as the temple is situated between twin volcanoes, Mount Merbabu and Merapi, making it a volatile area. Although many believe this was when the temple was abandoned, it is still mentioned in several documents as late as the 1400s. Others believe that its abandonment was due to the population converting to Islam in the fifteenth century. Over time, it was viewed as unwise, even taboo, to visit the temple. There are stories chronicled in Javanese literature dating back to the eighteenth century that associate visiting it with bad luck and curses. An insurgent of rebels against the King of Matram were defeated on the site in 1709; they were then captured and sentenced to death. Later, a prince came to the temple,

Kamadhatu realm

Rupadhatu realm

Arupadhatu realm

N

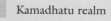
50 m
50 yds

**Borobudur Temple,
Indonesia**

despite being warned not to, as he desired to look at a statue inside one of the stupas, that he described, perhaps strangely. as 'a knight in a cage'. Nobody knows why he was so drawn to the temple or why he favoured this particular statue with sympathy, but it is written that after his visit, he took ill and died the following day. The people of Java knew a sacred building lay abandoned in the jungle, and it became increasingly mired in mystery. Once a great place of worship to rival any in the world, it was now consumed by ash and vines.

According to the 'Gunadharma Legend', the temple's origins lie in a gravely ill queen of the land being advised by a wise counsellor, possibly a holy mystic, that if she vowed to build a great temple, she would be cured of her ailment. She did so, and consequently made a full recovery, upon which she asked her son, later King Samaratungga, to build the temple – and so it stands today.

It is unsurprising that such a grand sacred monument is subject to folklore – even its architecture is a culmination of geomancy that is designed to enlighten those who pass through and around its many corridors and pathways, taking them to a higher state of being and elevated consciousness. This temple was built not only as a shrine to a deity but to the ability one can achieve when 'enlightened'. This positive sense of power can become inverted and when such sacred places are desecrated or abandoned, they tend to keep their sense of power in local beliefs but become warped into negative associations.

This is reflected in the local belief that the temple is connected to what is now known as the Waisak festival – during which Indonesian people celebrate the birth, enlightenment and death of the Buddha. It is believed that walking the specific clockwise pathway here connects one

to cosmic power, and that the stupas are a form of spiritual technology designed to harness energies. When one emerges from the dark interior galleries into the light of the open upper level, it is believed they are transformed metaphysically.

If the architecture is designed to be supernatural in nature and alter one's consciousness or elevate one's metaphysical state, then what happens to it when it lies empty and dormant? Does that power become inverted? Also, can the positive pathway here be altered or does it become a negative force when actions that stand in opposition of its theological countenance are enacted (the bloodshed of a war, the theft of sacred objects etc.)? Perhaps this is where the earlier stories of bad luck and superstition came from. Psychologically, we give power to places of worship, but that power can become fear of darker forces when we see those places in physical darkness and ruin.

And yet, despite volcanic activity and the human threats of destruction the temple has seen over the years, including terror bombings as recent as the 1980s, it now stands strong, helping millions of pilgrims, each seeking the elusive high astral state of nirvana, on their journey each year.

LEFT TOP: Detailed architecture designed to take visitors on a path through three spiritual realms.
ABOVE: Stupas atop the Borobudur Temple complex.

Duzgun Baba

Sacred mountain of the Alevi shepherd saint

In the Tunceli Province of eastern Türkiye, there stands a mountain named after a shepherd saint, where people travel to place goat horns upon a rock shrine and worship as part of one of the smallest religious groups in the world, Alevism. There is an aspect of Islam known as Sufism; this is an interaction between older mystical beliefs often viewed as Pagan and pre-existing Islamic systems, which give rise to a form of Islam where Muslims focus on searching for God within, shunning materialism. Both Islam and its Sufi derivate influenced Alevism, a mystical-type religion that is essentially rooted in worshipping the same figures found in Islam, particularly Ali, but which also draws on Zoroastrianism, Armenian mythology and shamanism. The Alevis focus on tolerance and love, and for some this includes the worship of nature, yet they have been persecuted and suffered massacres through the ages. Here in the Tunceli Province you would find Turkish Alevis and Kurdish Alevis, who make up an estimated 4–25 per cent of the religious population of Turkey as a whole. But there is a minority even within this minority – the Zaza Alevis. It is these people who you will meet on the sacred mountain of Duzgun Baba.

Known locally as the Kirmanc, these people speak a dialect that is different from all other Kurds found in Türkiye, and worship in a way unique to them that connects their natural surroundings to their divinity. The traditions are passed down orally, and instead of having strict religious rules to follow, they tend to recite spiritual poetry, including a form of prayer to the sun and moon. To them all animals and beings are sacred, but especially the mountain goat, as the goats are the property of saints. Local legend goes that Duzgan Baba, who at the time was a shepherd by the name Sah Haydar, was known for having very well-fed goats even during wintertime when food supplies were scarce. His father, an important religious leader, became curious as to how he managed this, so one day, he followed his son up the mountain. There he saw that anywhere the young shepherd touched his staff, suddenly flourished into greenery and the goats were able to graze happily. His father was both stunned and proud, but before he could make his presence known to his son, one of the goats in the flock sneezed and his son said to it, 'What's the matter? Can you smell my father, *Kureso Khurr*?', a nickname for his father considered taboo in a society that reveres its elders. The young shepherd turned around and, seeing that his father was indeed standing

there, he suddenly bolted to the top of the mountain, where he disappeared into another realm out of shame. From then on, he was known as Duzgun Baba, and the mountain was named after him.

The Zaza Alevis believe that the mountain goats found here are his disbanded flock, still looking for their shepherd. Part of the way up the mountain there is a cave, just narrow enough to crawl into, said to be the sleeping quarters of Duzgun Baba when he worked on the mountain. It is held as a sacred place where some travel to spend the night, hoping to be visited by the saint. At the very top is a large sacred mound made up of individual stones (the equivalent of a Scottish 'cairn', used to mark burial sites and landmarks), which denotes the symbolic grave of Duzgun Baba.

These stones are not the only sacred rocks here. Further down at the bottom of the mountain there is a small area, a base really for those making the ascent up the mountain. Between some small benches and resting places lies a large boulder, which is adorned with many goat horns and some with ribbons. This stone is used for offerings to deities and gods and is also a shrine to the Alevi saint. There is also a *cemevi* – a hall that the Zaza Alevis worship in.

The etymology of different saints and gods here is complex, and you may see the mountain shepherd saint called Duzgin Bawo as the word 'Duzgun' is a Turkish interpretation of the Alevi mythology. Duzgin Bawo / Duzgun Baba is believed to be based on Tuzik, a deity whose name means 'sharp' in Zazaki and is the embodiment of a mountain. This figure is connected to Vahagn, the god of fire and slayer of dragons from Armenian Zoroastrianism. This is likely due to the fact that Armenians resisted Christianization and continued to practise Zoroastrianism while living up in the mountains along this region. Duzgin Bawo/Duzgun Baba is said to settle conflicts and when two Zaza or Kurdish Alevis cannot resolve a dispute themselves, they make a pilgrimage to the top of the mountain to seek his help. A person may also travel to the top to make a plea for a son and you will find women worshipping him in a way that reflects a fertility god. The mountain itself is also connected to healing as Duzgun/Duzgin had a sister called Xaskar. She is now revered as a water goddess and there is a water source named after her. It is said that if only those who are good and pure of heart drink from it, then the water will never dry up.

RIGHT TOP: The sacred cave that was his resting place.

RIGHT BOTTOM: The shrine to Duzgun Baba covered in goat horns.

Luxor Temple

Sacred temple where kings were bound to ancient gods

The Egyptian city of Luxor, as we know it today, is the site of royalty, divinity and the afterlife.

Once known as the legendary City of Thebes, it is described as 'the world's greatest open-air museum', due to its ancient architecture and colossal monuments. Across the bank of the Nile River lies the city's Theban Necropolis, where ritual burials were conducted. It was divided into the 'Valley of the Kings' for the pharaohs and the 'Valley of the Queens' for their wives. Not only royalty is connected to this city, but the gods and goddesses themselves. Before Luxor was Thebes and the capital city of Upper Egypt during the New Kingdom (sixteenth to eleventh centuries BCE), it was the City of Amun. The patron deity of Thebes a little more than 4,000 years ago, Amun was a 'tutelary' deity, one who protects and safeguards what it represents. Both Amun and his wife, Amaunet, are mentioned in the pyramid texts written in Old Egyptian, which are the oldest religious texts in all of Egypt. Amun would later become fused with the sun god Ra to become Amun-Ra, now arguably the most recognized Egyptian god. It wasn't the first time Thebes had been a central place for worshipping sun gods: Amun-Ra replaced Montu as their patron deity – the Egyptian god of war, a manifestation of the sun's scorching and destructive rays and depicted with the head of a falcon.

Amun-Ra has one of the greatest temples dedicated to him; it is a precinct surrounded by a sacred lake that forms part of the massive Karnak Temple Complex. This epic site on the East Bank was once connected to another temple by a processional walkway lined with Sphinx statues – the temple known now as Luxor Temple. This great walkway was finally completely excavated and restored in 2021 with a spectacular ceremony to reopen it. The temple was constructed by several different rulers, including Ramesses II and Tutankhamun. In Egyptian the temple is known as *Ipet-resyt*, translating as 'the southern sanctuary'. This is a reference to its location: it's southern-orientated towards Karnak Temple, an unusual feature since most Egyptian temples are built on an east–west axis. This not only mimics the path of the sun rising in the east and setting in the west but honours the spiritual significance of life arriving on one side and departing on the other in a cosmological balance. This is why the tombs of the pharaohs and their wives are on the West Bank:

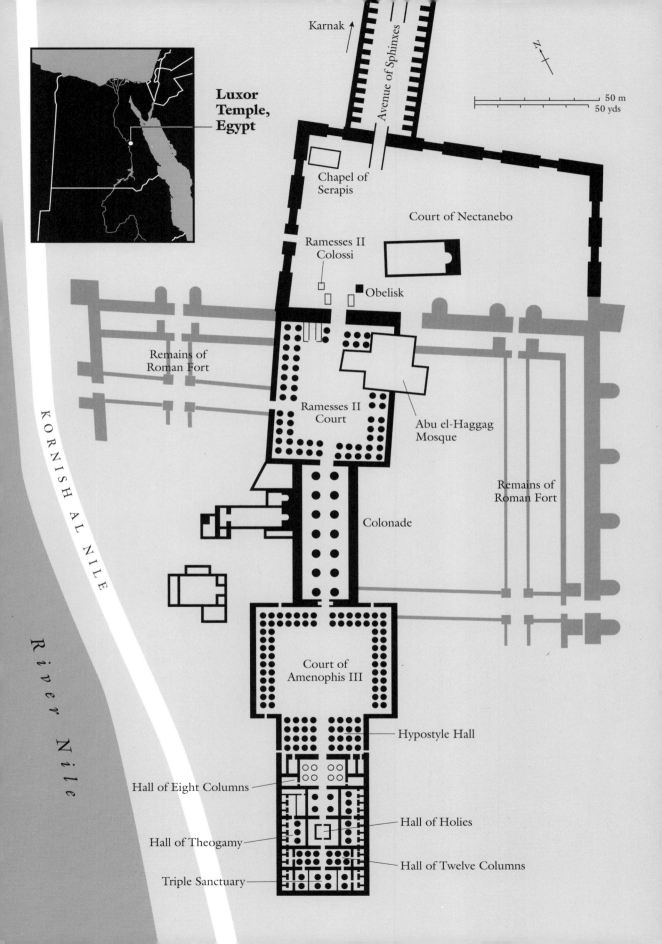

Karnak ↑

Avenue of Sphinxes

N

50 m
50 yds

Luxor
Temple,
Egypt

Chapel of
Serapis

Court of Nectanebo

Ramesses II
Colossi

Obelisk

Remains of
Roman Fort

Ramesses II
Court

Abu el-Haggag
Mosque

Remains of
Roman Fort

Colonade

KORNISH AL NILE

Court of
Amenophis III

Hypostyle Hall

Hall of Eight Columns

Hall of Holies

Hall of Theogamy

Hall of Twelve Columns

Triple Sanctuary

River Nile

the sun 'dies' each day on the western horizon and therefore this is the place that holds the dead.

Luxor Temple was home to the ancient ceremony known as Opet, held in the second month of the lunar calendar. This was a time when the cult statues of Amun-Ra were carried over from the sister temple at Karnak in a large wooden boat, called the 'procession of the barque'. The 'barque' was a large vessel carved from cedar wood and covered in gold, adorned with a sacred ram's head. Once at the temple the statues were placed inside a 'birthing chamber' and there the current presiding pharaoh would take part in a type of marriage ritual where they were joined spiritually with Amun-Ra. This was followed by a recrowning ceremony that reinforced the fertility of the pharaoh and their divine right as ruler and intermediary between the gods and the people of Egypt. The ritual sometimes lasted for weeks on end and many great feasts were held here celebrating a unification point where god and man are one.

Throughout the centuries almost every pharaoh added statues, columns and shrines to different gods to the temple. Even after the Greeks arrived, Alexander the Great rebuilt the Chapel of Amun and had himself depicted as an Egyptian pharaoh. When the Romans arrived, their leader, Hadrian, built a shrine to Serapis – the Graeco-Egyptian deity who was created by combining Osiris (the Egyptian god of the dead), Apis (the sacred bull deity that symbolized the king), Hades (the Greek king of the Underworld) and Dionysus (the Greek god of wine and festivities). Later, the Roman Empire constructed Christian churches around the temple, which became mosques when Egypt was conquered by the Arabs. Irrespective of architecture, Luxor Temple has a rare supernatural quality because it wasn't just a place of worship, an act often viewed as passive, but a place where a king was supposed to meet their god and be bound to them, an active and transformative act. Many people visit sites where acts of ritualistic magic took place and believe that they still hold power. If you believe that, it should come as no surprise that places such as Luxor continue to hold supernatural influence, and that influence transcends borders. In 1936, Sir Alexander Hay Seton, the 10th Baronet Seton, visited Egypt with his wife, Zeyla, and after visiting the temples of Luxor, a local guide offered to take them into a newly opened tomb that was being excavated. The tomb predated the act of mummification and held a skeleton on a slab that had been partly destroyed by flooding from the Nile. During this secret visit, Zeyla stole a small bone from the skeleton of an upper-class Egyptian female, believed to be a princess. Upon returning to Edinburgh, the Setons showed it to friends they were hosting for supper, after which it was placed in a small box and left on the dining room table. Shortly afterwards, as the guests were leaving, there was an almighty crash and part of the roof parapet caved in, landing just a few feet away from the startled guests: it would have killed them had they been struck. The case with the bone in it was moved to a side table. A few nights later, their nanny came rushing upstairs in the middle of the night to say she'd heard someone in the dining room but the Baronet found nobody there. In the morning, however, they found the side table on its side, with the case and bone lying on the floor next to it. They began hearing footsteps on the stairs and were continually woken up by the sounds of someone moving around the house when no one was there.

The bone was moved to the drawing room. Soon after, a nephew came to stay and reported seeing a strange person walking up the stairs in the night (when he got up to use the bathroom). The Baronet became concerned they were being robbed and elected to stay up all night watching the house. He locked the drawing room and checked all the windows, and, with the key in his pocket, he eventually went to bed after no disturbance had occurred. He was woken by his wife and nanny yelling about someone being downstairs. He rushed down, armed with a revolver, and had to fetch the key to unlock the drawing room. Once inside, he described it as looking like 'a battle royal' had taken place – chairs were upended, books had been flung about, and in the middle of all the chaos, was the stolen bone. Fearing that it was this object causing the trouble, they moved all the contents of the drawing room, including the bone, downstairs to a different room and the same thing occurred there. The room with the bone was completely trashed from the inside despite being locked, with no alternative entry. At one point they came home to find that the heavy table the bone had sat on was now cracked, as if an immense pressure had been placed upon it. When the bone was moved back to the drawing room, the banging and noises continued and when they opened it, the table was completely smashed – the bone itself broken into five pieces. It was mended as best as possible, and they had a medical friend examine it to determine that it was a sacrum bone. Things seemed to calm down until Boxing Day. While hosting friends, the table with the bone on it, despite nobody being near it, completely lifted and hurled itself into the wall on the opposite side of the room. Several people who had been visiting fainted.

By this point stories spread and it hit the papers, even reaching American publications. Among the thousands of letters received, one came from Dr Carter, the famous excavator of the tomb of Tutankhamen. He advised that this type of supernatural occurrence was indeed possible and would simply keep on going. The Baronet decided to destroy the bone by having it burnt. Although he stated there was peace for a while, ultimately, he felt that the bone's impact lingered, as his marriage ended, his daughter and wife became very ill, his own health began to fail and 'altogether life was very difficult'.

The number of objects taken from Egyptian sacred sites such as Luxor over the years, was high, at one point even leading to British fields being fertilized with the remains of mummified cats because so many were taken from Egypt and brought back to the UK. With such powerful rites conducted in sites such as Luxor, where kings were bound to ancient gods, it is perhaps inevitable that disturbing the remains and stealing artefacts that are supposed to accompany the dead into their afterlife have resulted in paranormal disturbances. Good advice might be: if you visit such sacred places, keep your hands firmly in your own pockets.

PREVIOUS LEFT: Colossal statues of Ramsses II at the entrance to Luxor Temple.
LEFT: Entrance to Luxor Temple, known as the 'world's greatest open air museum'.
ABOVE: Members of a family walk along the Avenue of the Sphinxes near the Coptic Orthodox Church of the Virgin Mary.
NEXT: Avenue of Sphinxes restored in remembrance of the inaugural Opet Festival.

Chapter 4

Myths &
Legends

Čachtice Castle

Castle that was once the prison of the 'Bloody Countess' Elizabeth Báthory

This infamous castle was built in the mid-thirteenth century, up in the Little Carpathians, a mountain range overlooking the village of Čachtice, in what is today Slovakia. Now a ruin, it was formally devised to be a sentry on the route to the historical region of Moravia in the east of the Czech Republic. Built by Kazimir from the Hunt-Poznan Clan, it passed through many noble and aristocratic families over the years, including the controversial Matthew III Csák – a Hungarian Palatine who independently ruled the north western territories of medieval Hungary and was vastly romanticized as a national hero of Slovak history. In the late sixteenth century, the castle finally came to be in the possession of a woman fabled to be the most prolific and disturbed female serial killer in history – Countess Elizabeth Báthory. Reported to have murdered more than 600 young women in the Castle, Báthory's actions earned Čachtice the reputation of being one of one of the most haunted destinations in Europe. Countess Elizabeth Báthory de Ecsed (born Báthori Erzsébet) was a Hungarian noblewoman born in 1560 to Baron György Báthory of Ecsed and Baroness Anna Báthory of Somlya. During her youth, she suffered from what was known as a 'falling sickness', or what we would now call epilepsy. At the time it was often treated by pouring the blood of someone without the condition upon the lips of the epileptic sufferer. This was later cited as influencing the heinous crimes she is alleged to have committed.

Understanding how the grim folklore of Countess Báthory came to be requires a dive into the political, religious and socioeconomic circumstances of her time. At just ten years old, Báthory was engaged to marry Ferenc II Nádasdy, a marriage of political convenience and scheming crafted by Ferenc's mother to bring together two of the most powerful families in the land, and resulting in a combined land ownership that spanned across Transylvania and Hungary. They were married in 1575 when Ferenc was nineteen and Báthory was fifteen. As Báthory's family had stood in power longer and had a more noble lineage, her maiden name was also adopted by her husband. As a wedding gift, she was bestowed Čachtice Castle and many of its surrounding villages. Just a few years after their union, Ferenc took charge of the Hungarian forces and led them to war against the Ottoman Empire. It became Báthory's duty to manage the estates in her husband's absence as they were, too, under great threat of invasion. She also was tasked with providing medical aid and relief to the villages they owned.

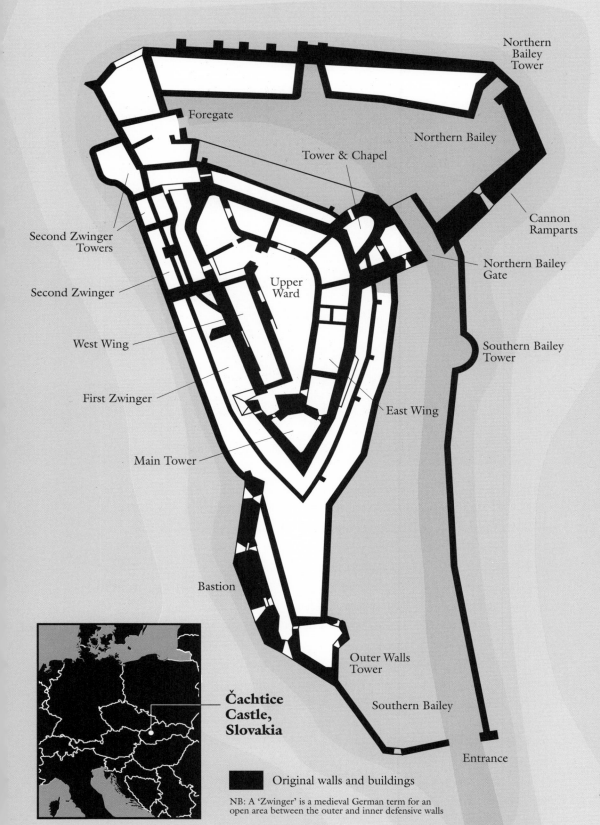

25 m
25 yds

Northern Bailey Tower

Foregate

Northern Bailey

Tower & Chapel

Second Zwinger Towers

Cannon Ramparts

Second Zwinger

Northern Bailey Gate

West Wing

Upper Ward

Southern Bailey Tower

First Zwinger

East Wing

Main Tower

Bastion

Outer Walls Tower

Southern Bailey

Čachtice Castle, Slovakia

Entrance

N

Original walls and buildings

NB: A 'Zwinger' is a medieval German term for an open area between the outer and inner defensive walls

Unlike her husband, who was barely literate in his native Hungarian tongue and only passable with Latin and German, Báthory was one of the most educated women in all the land and spoke multiple languages. This helped her rule efficiently and navigate the Ottoman–Hungarian wars. It is also important to note that Báthory was a life-long Calvinist and though her husband was Lutheran in faith she never converted. It is well documented that she was not only tolerant of her subjects of Lutheran faith but actively financed the building of their schools and education of their ministers – she believed in religious freedom in her lands.

The descent from high nobility to fabled madness and cruelty began in the years running up to her husband's death. As the stories were passed down through generations – including ones of her bathing and drinking in the blood of her victims to keep herself young – they were no doubt exaggerated, and yet the horrific crimes that Báthory is said to have committed have influenced everything from cinema to music. But is any of it true?

One theory is that the decimation of the Countess's reputation was to do with a power grab. In the run-up to Ferenc's death, there was an increasing desire by the Habsburg Empire to expand into independent Transylvania. They already had power over Hungary

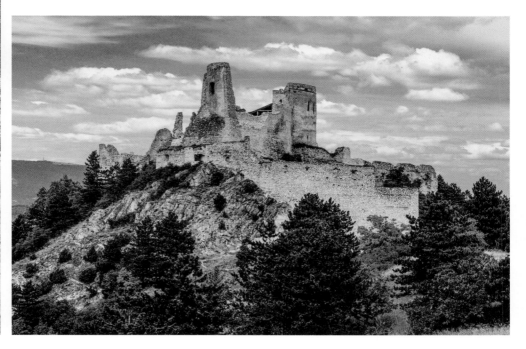

but they struggled to gain control, as the Prince of Transylvania, Gabor Báthory, also had designs on taking the Hungarian throne. So the Hapsburgs set about trying to destroy the lineage to ensure the Báthory family would be stripped of its nobility, wealth and power status. At the time, Elizabeth Báthory lived in Hungary, which was ruled by King Mathias II, whose throne was under threat from Gabor Báthory, and this made her their primary target. When her husband, Ferenc, died after battling an illness that affected his mobility, Countess Báthory's property and wealth became combined with that of the Nádasdy family, making her the owner of one of the largest estates in all the land. Most notably her ownership of Čachtice Castle created a problem because it was in a strategic location that could be used to aid Gabor Báthory if he pursued the Hungarian throne. This formed the backdrop to the Countess's trial.

György Thurzó was the Palatine of Hungary at this time and he thought if they could get rid of Elizabeth Báthory, on charges so heinous that her whole lineage would be disgraced and forced to flee the country, then his own son could be placed as Prince of Transylvania. Thurzó started a vicious rumour campaign that Báthory had torture dungeons in every one of her properties and that she used these to torture and kill young women. He especially

cited the locations that would be of strategic importance to the Habsburg Empire (such as Čachtice Castle). Before arriving at any of these locations to investigate the supposed crimes and wrangle witnesses, they spread the rumours and horror stories thoroughly so that every 'witness' was now regurgitating the same lines and they could be used to confirm Báthory's guilt. Three hundred witnesses to the Countess's alleged crimes testified at her trial, but curiously none of them were injured themselves, nor had they seen the acts with their own eyes, and they reported death numbers with wildly varying degrees – some saying she killed a dozen, some saying she killed hundreds of young girls.

Part of Báthory's duties was overseeing medical care for women in her villages, which required having staff trained in herbal medicine, and often bringing young girls to her own properties for the treatment of various ailments. Most of her medical practice was grounded in traditional east Hungarian methods, often seen as foreign and strange to west Hungarians. She also had a Croatian midwife and healer on staff who was trained in surgical practices. The surgical treatments could range from blood-letting (a practice where patients were covered in leeches or small cuts were made in order to drain blood from the wounded site, believing it would also drain the illness and infection with it), through to basic surgical interventions. Such methods roused further suspicion because surgical practices were reserved only for male doctors. Thus, rumours of black magic and the surgeries as forms of torture were easy to plant in susceptible people's minds.

Reading through the witness testimonies, it is possible to see that their descriptions of the horrible tortures might actually be surgical procedures. Among other things, Báthory was accused of dunking women from cold water to hot water (sometimes done with plague victims in a bid to activate what we would now call an immune response), piercing their tongues with spikes (lancing boils in the mouth?) and inserting pokers into the vagina of young girls (possibly an early form of speculum to investigate venereal disease). The recorded deaths also coincided with outbreaks of various diseases and epidemics, most notably typhus and the bubonic plague.

One week in October of 1610 saw eight girls die at one of Báthory's properties after showing symptoms of disease. The healer tending them at the time, aware of the rumours swirling, panicked and buried the bodies around the estate. At the time, Báthory was away travelling with her daughter and when she returned, she had the shocking and gruesome experience of finding one of the bodies when her dog dug it up in the estate. Once the death had been officially recorded, Thurzó planned to turn up at the castle unannounced and arrest Báthory. She was never read formal charges or given a summons. Thurzó is often cited in the folktales as catching Báthory right in the act of murdering a girl when he turned up at the castle with no prior warning, when actually historic documents state that she was eating supper at the time. Her servants were tortured for information on the other bodies, one of which was exhumed in the courtyard and due to the cool weather and favourable ground conditions had been quite well preserved. Thurzó claimed this was the fresh corpse of the woman Báthory had been torturing to death when he arrived to arrest her.

During this circus of a trial, the Countess was never allowed to defend herself or give contrary evidence. Instead, she was publicly discredited and her servants were tortured into giving false testimonies, then executed as accomplices. Báthory herself was imprisoned for life in the tower of Čachtice Castle, where she lived for four years before her death in August of 1614. But the persecution of her extended past her death. In 1729, a Jesuit priest wrote about the case of Countess Báthory as a cautionary tale and part of counter-Reformation propaganda. He stated she was a Catholic who had become a wild murderess after converting to Lutheranism, which we know never happened as she remained a devout Calvinist all her life. However, the tales of her alleged crimes were so entrenched in public knowledge by this point that it allowed this piece of propaganda to become the backbone of the mythology surrounding the 'Bloody Countess'. The priest described how Báthory murdered hundreds of young girls in order to drain them of their blood so that she might bathe in it to preserve her own youth and beauty.

This moment would create a long legacy of Countess Elizabeth Báthory. She became known as 'the female Dracula' and her story was fed into the area's already saturated vampire lore. The castle itself would later become the backdrop of the iconic 1922 horror film *Nosferatu*. In the book *Guinness World Records*, Elizabeth Báthory is still listed as the female serial killer with the highest number of victims ever recorded in history. And yet, if any of it is true, how many of her victims still roam Čachtice Castle and its grounds?

LEFT: Countess Elizabeth Báthory de Ecsed (7 August 1560 – 21 August 1614).
NEXT: The old ruins of Castle Čachtice that became the prison of the infamous 'blood countess'.

Cortijo Jurado

Rural Spanish murder house connected to satanic cultists

This infamous Gothic revival-style *cortijo* (the rural Spanish equivalent of a farmhouse) was built in the nineteenth century by the wealthy and influential Heredia family in the Málaga province of Spain, out on the outskirts known as the Campanillas district. It has long been associated with evil, including the disappearance of several young girls in the area, whose bodies were found near the river, not far from the *cortijo,* mutilated and rumoured to be the victims of satanic rituals carried out there. Their spirits are meant to haunt the area.

Built on more than 45,000 sq m (484,000 sq ft) of land, it was converted in hopes of becoming a sprawling agricultural enterprise but now sits derelict and foreboding. In 1925, the property was sold to another bourgeois family, the Larios, and its legacy continued this way until it finally came to be owned by the Jurado family in 1975. In 2000, the building and land was bought by a development company seeking to build a 4-star hotel there, but the project endured scandal, lawsuits and numerous permit problems – it has still not been built to this day. The mansion is also known to some as Casa Encantada, likely in reference to the famous property of the same name that is located in Bel Air, Los Angeles, which holds the record for the most expensive home ever sold in America.

The bones of Cortijo Jurado still jut out on the hill above a busy road on the outskirts of Málaga but it's more than just a testament to the decay of fortunes – it sits at the core of local ghost stories, bizarre disappearances and cult phenomena. Some believe that the legend really began when the patriarchal figurehead of the Heredia family died, but it's likely that rumours began even before that as the secret lives of the super wealthy are always subject to speculation and gossip. The fundamental horror of the legend lies in the disappearances of many young women in the area between the years of 1890 and 1920, whose bodies were rumoured to show signs of ritualistic abuse and violent murder.

The Heredia family became the primary suspects in these acts, and it is believed that they were kidnapping, torturing, abusing and then murdering young women in dark rituals. The house itself is a bizarre mash-up of classical Spanish architecture, British neo-Gothic revivalism and Scandinavian influences. One of its most striking features is its windows – it has 365 of them, one for every day of the year. But the aspect most talked about is its deep basements and tunnels. Many say that the young women were lured into the property or

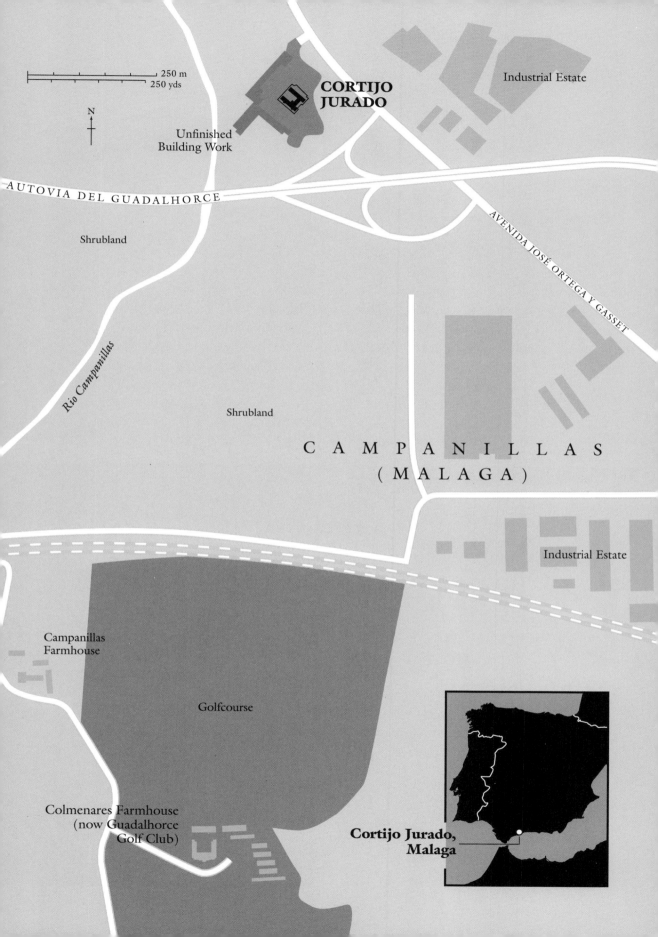

250 m
250 yds

N

**CORTIJO
JURADO**

Industrial Estate

Unfinished
Building Work

AUTOVIA DEL GUADALHORCE

Shrubland

AVENIDA JOSÉ ORTEGA Y GASSET

Rio Campanillas

Shrubland

C A M P A N I L L A S
(M A L A G A)

Industrial Estate

Campanillas
Farmhouse

Golfcourse

Colmenares Farmhouse
(now Guadalhorce
Golf Club)

**Cortijo Jurado,
Malaga**

LEFT TOP The decaying exterior of Cortijo Jurado.

LEFT BOTTOM: Graffiti inside the abandoned house.

LEFT: This crumbling manor became connected to cultists and stories of torture.

kidnapped and transported via these tunnels. This part of the story is in fact verifiable insofar that the tunnels really do exist; even more importantly, they connect to another nearby mansion, one that was owned by the Lario family, who also came to be the second owners of this 'murder house'. Speculation states that the Larios and Heredias had a pact and were conspiring together over satanic rituals and violent murder, either as an act of collective fetish or as part of a wider religious cult movement

There is an account by a former worker of the property, Manuel Martin, who says that he entered the property via one of these tunnels in the 1940s after hearing the rumours and found human bones and what appeared to be torture devices. The underground areas can still be accessed via the stall of the farm itself but in the 1950s the owners closed it with a cement wall.

The legends have drawn ghost hunters, mediums and journalists alike to explore the property. There are recordings of what are claimed to be EVPs (electronic voice phenomena) taken at the property, where voices mutter and moan to one another from thin air. There are also testimonies of phantom figures spotted in the courtyard outside, where some have said they heard ghostly voices tell them there are bodies buried directly beneath.

Paranormal enthusiasts aren't the only ones to have strange experiences as Jorge Rivera tried to direct a film about the ultra-racist cosmological horror writer H.P. Lovecraft here, but the production was plagued with accidents, fires, equipment drainage and even a lead actor falling down an elevator shaft and then seemingly vanishing into the unknown after he was released from hospital. The film was never completed but has certainly amplified the legends of this Spanish haunted house. Truth and fiction blending perhaps into supernatural urban legend?

Goblin Ha'

Castle belonging to legendary wizard who advised King Alexander III

This little ruined castle buried in a forest in East Lothian, Scotland, is a relic of both history and folklore. Its actual title is Yester Castle but it is better known locally as Goblin Ha' (*Ha'* being the Scots word for hall) due to its unusual construction, and fabled ties to the creatures we call goblins; the hall itself is the main structure that remains of it. The land was granted to a Norman immigrant by the name of Hugh de Giffard I at the behest of King William the Lion – the nearby town of Gifford takes its name from this feudal family. Yester later fell to his grandson Sir Hugh Giffard II, or Hugo de Gifford, who would become a legendary character in Scottish lore and give Goblin Ha' the reputation it has today. Gifford was a renowned wizard, known for his supernatural practices, often carried out in the lower regions of the castle. Yester Castle was built between 1250 and 1267 – or as some rumour would have it – summoned into being by supernatural creatures. It was later destroyed in the fourteenth century and when being rebuilt the only original feature retained was the infamous Goblin Ha'. In order to gain entrance into this hall you must pass through a tiny doorway that is easy to miss as it's just a few feet high – some believe the approximate height of a goblin. It is the only entrance and exit to the hall. Inside is a grand banquet hall with a vaulted ceiling, two unusual windows and a single passageway. The passageway is a set of winding stone steps that go downwards into the earth – and then stop, as if they began constructing a passageway to something else below and then ceased abruptly. Entering that hall at a forced stoop through the tiny, pitch black, narrow, passage is unsettling – even more so at night.

Whether the stairway to nothing – or 'gateway to hell', as it's sometimes referred to – was intentional or simply unfinished remains perplexing. What were they trying to achieve with this subterranean stairway? Excavating beneath the castle to create a new space would have been incredibly difficult and structurally unsound. The lack of decent building records in the 1200s made it hard to ascertain whether there was a structure underneath first, so many accepted the fabled hall to be the large one that remains and the stairway to nothing a strange addition. In an 1855 edition of the book *Marmion*, in which Hugo is immortalized, Sir Walter Scott gives in the footnotes a mixture of first-hand accounts of the building and some additional notes provided by historical documents composed by Sir David Dalrymple,

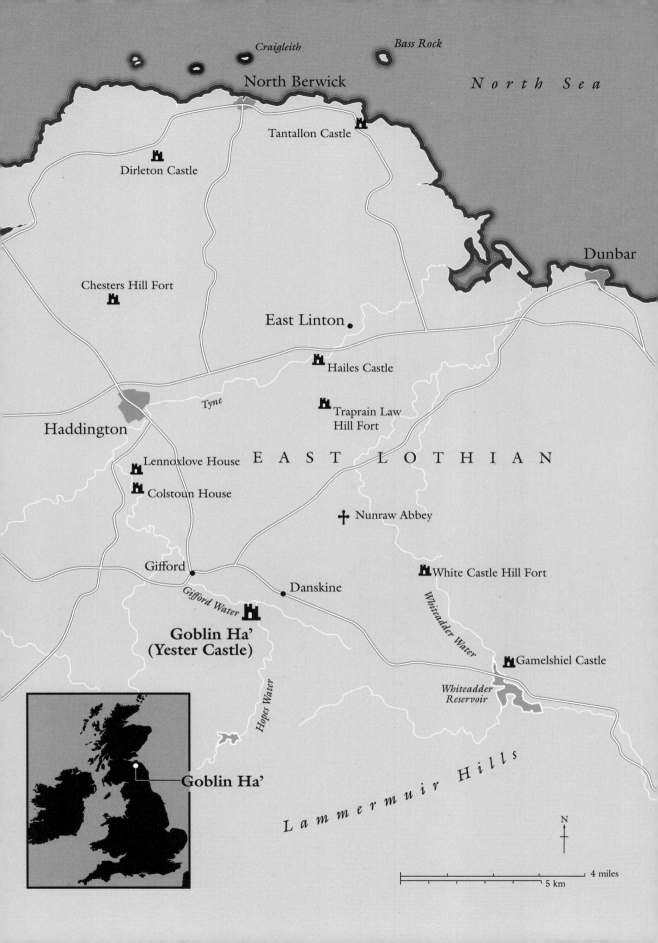

Craigleith

Bass Rock

North Sea

North Berwick

Tantallon Castle

Dirleton Castle

Dunbar

Chesters Hill Fort

East Linton

Hailes Castle

Tyne

Traprain Law
Hill Fort

Haddington

E A S T   L O T H I A N

Lennoxlove House

Colstoun House

Nunraw Abbey

Gifford

White Castle Hill Fort

Danskine

Gifford Water

Whiteadder Water

Goblin Ha'
(Yester Castle)

Gamelshiel Castle

Hopes Water

*Whiteadder
Reservoir*

Goblin Ha'

N

L a m m e r m u i r   H i l l s

4 miles

5 km

both of which give us some fresh clues. It is written that beneath the castle was 'a capacious cavern formed by magical art and called in the country Bo Hall (meaning Hobgoblin Hall)'. This is presumably the large, vaulted room that remains today, which we don't think of as being beneath anything because the top of the castle has been destroyed. It is also reported that 'a stair of thirty-six steps leads down to a pit which hath a communication with Hopes-water': this is the area that is now sadly lost due to the collapsed stairway. Scott closes his footnotes by saying that the hall is inaccessible due to the collapse of the stairs. So perhaps the tiny entrance to the remaining structure is not the initial, intended one. Perhaps it had a different purpose. It has served to embellish the goblin tales though. And yet the supernatural tales predate the destruction of the castle so this does not entirely solve the mystery of why we attribute its construction to paranormal methods. In fact there are conflicting accounts.

Hugo himself became known throughout history as a necromancer, a wizard and a confidant of King Alexander III and consort of many important figures in Scotland's history. This bizarre, legendary man later appears in Sir Walter Scott's *Marmion*, first published in 1808. King Alexander II of Scotland, notable for concluding the Treaty of York, which defined the border between England and Scotland and has remained relatively unchanged to this day, had only one son, Alaxandair mac Alaxandair. At the King's passing his crown was handed down and his son became King Alexander III of Scots at just seven years old. Due to his incredibly young age several notable figures were put in charge to guide the young king and be his counsel, including Hugo de Gifford. Alexander III famously died after falling from his horse in a terrible storm while riding through the night from Edinburgh to Fife to visit his new wife on her birthday. His death plunged Scotland into a period of great uncertainty and trouble as the land was left without a king for many years.

In *Marmion*, the knights are told a tale of Hugo de Gifford's time with Alexander III, where it is said that on the eve of battle against Haakon of Norway for the claim to the Outer Hebrides islands, Alexander III sought out Hugo. The wizard tells Alexander that if he wishes to know the outcome of the battle, he may fight a high elf who has the power to see into the future; if he succeeds fighting the mythological being, then the battle will be successful. Regardless of this fabled account, Alexander III really did challenge Haakon for the right to the western isles, although he rejected the claim and proceeded to invade Scotland from the west coast. The Norwegian king was defeated largely due to difficulty fighting in a storm that damaged many of his ships and he later died at Orkney trying to get home. The lands are still part of Scotland to this day. There is indisputable proof that King Alexander III was definitely at Yester Castle on 24 May, 1278, because he wrote a letter to King Edward I of England, while there. Through Scott's epic account we are able to get a glimpse of Hugo de Gifford in all his glory:

Lord Gifford deep beneath the ground heard Alexander's bugle sound, and tarried not his garb to change, but, in his wizard habit strange, came forth, a quaint and fearful sight: His mantle lined with fox-skins white; His high and wrinkled forehead bore a pointed cap, such as of yore clerk's say Pharoh's Magi wore; His shoes were marked with cross and spell, upon his breast a pentacle. His zone, of virgin parchment thin, or, as some tell, of dead man's skin,

his breast a pentacle. His zone, of virgin parchment thin, or, as some tell, of dead man's skin, bore many a planetary sign. Combust, and retrograde, and trine; and in his hand he held prepared, a naked sword without a guard.

The description here gives us a clear and potent image of a man practising ritual magic, but even prior to this we get a glimpse at his legendary powers through a description of the castle being built, in which Scott states that not a single mortal arm helped to build the place and that it was all done under '*word and charm*'. This implies that Hugo used magic to construct the place but rather than it simply being brought forth out of the elements, or birthed into existence from seemingly thin air, he enchanted a magical workforce to build it at his command. He goes on to lament that his grandparents told stories of hearing the clamour and noise of the construction as far away as Dunbar, and that it was brought about by '*those dread artizans of hell, who labour'd under Hugo's spell.*'

This is how Yester Castle came to be known as Goblin Hall or Goblin Ha'. But what exactly constitutes a goblin? It is defined broadly as a 'small, grotesque, creature' that is featured primarily in the folklore of various European cultures. It is said that these creatures can become nasty and cause items to disappear, sour milk, and injure pets and farm animals. Ones that are connected to marshlands or holes in the ground take on more sinister acts and are said to abduct children. 'Goblin' is sometimes used as an umbrella term for all fae creatures (types of spirit that are connected to fairy folk), which include not only Boggles but things like imps, gnomes and dwarves. This interchangeability is likely what has given rise to such variance in accounts of their appearance and skills. In the case of Goblin Ha', they are seemingly summoned from the depths of the forest, to build the castle. Scott describes them as the 'artizans of hell' and this links to a version of the lore in which Hugo de Gifford made a pact with the Devil to summon an army of Goblins.

Bringing forth these creatures wasn't the warlock's only legendary act of magic. Near to the village of Haddington lies Colstoun House, the ancestral home of the Broun Clan. When a member of this clan married Hugo's daughter, Margaret, they were given a pear that had been enchanted by Hugo and placed in a silver box. They were told that as long as this pear remained safe and untouched the family would prosper. The clan did indeed have good fortune, until 1692, when the fiancée of Sir George Broun, who had inherited the estate, decided to take the pear out from the silver box and, seeing that it looked as fresh as the day it was picked, couldn't resist taking a bite of it. The fortune soon disappeared and the family amassed large debt. When Sir George Broun died without producing a male heir, they were forced to sell the estate. The people they sold it to were killed while travelling to Edinburgh when a flash flood caused the River Tyne to burst its banks. It is said that the pear, now hard as stone with the bite mark still visible, is held at Colstoun House to this day.

PREVIOUS LEFT: Part of the remains of Yester Castle near Haddington in East Lothian, Scotland.
RIGHT: Inside the Goblin Ha' at Yester Castle.
NEXT: An old arched bridge over the Gifford Water.

Burg Eltz

*Fairytale castle where the ghost of a young woman still defends it
from an unwelcome lover*

This twelfth-century medieval German castle, perched above the Moselle River and
set within a small, wooded valley, is one of only three in the region to never have been
destroyed. A perfect fortress, its position makes it easy to defend. It has housed a branch of
the Eltz family for more than 800 years and remains a piece of history trapped in time. Like
all good castles, it has a ghost – that of a woman who defended her home from an unwanted
suitor and paid for her bravery with her life. Her ghost – and that of the suitor asking for
forgiveness – are said to roam the lands.

 With more than one hundred rooms, Burg Eltz required so many staff that it once had
a small village built below, where servants and craftspeople dedicated to the castle lived. It
lies on a rich trade route that was utilized during the western Roman Empire, but when it
fell in the fifth century BCE, the Franks took over and, as the land was divided, this area
was given to the son of King Charlemagne. At the time it was simply a manor hall that had
been constructed in the ninth century, which amazingly still stands today, but a few hundred
years later the House of Eltz began work on the site to bring it into a fortress state. Over
the centuries, many additions were made, including the 10-storey Greater Rodendorf House
that boasts high-vaulted, Gothic-style ceilings and a flag hall. The original main hall was
replaced in 1615 with what is now known as Kempenich House, a feat of architecture that
was ahead of its time, which allowed every single room to be heated. Many of these rooms
are still available to be viewed today in their opulent, original state.

 Remarkably the castle was never destroyed over the centuries, although it came very close
during the Nine Years' War (1688–97), when many early Rhenish castles were instructed to
be obliterated. Eltz was saved because its lord at the time was Hans Eltz-Uttingen, a senior
officer in the Royal French Army, and he used his position to have Burg Eltz deleted from
the list of buildings that soldiers were instructed to ruin. Despite never having endured the
constant violence and chaos of sieges that many other historic castles have experienced over
the years – acts that can often give rise to a mixture of paranormal activity and folklore –
Burg Eltz still has its fair share of ghosts.

 During the sixteenth century, the castle was home to Agnes Eltz, the sole female among
a large male family, and the daughter of the 15th Count of Eltz. Agnes defied gender roles

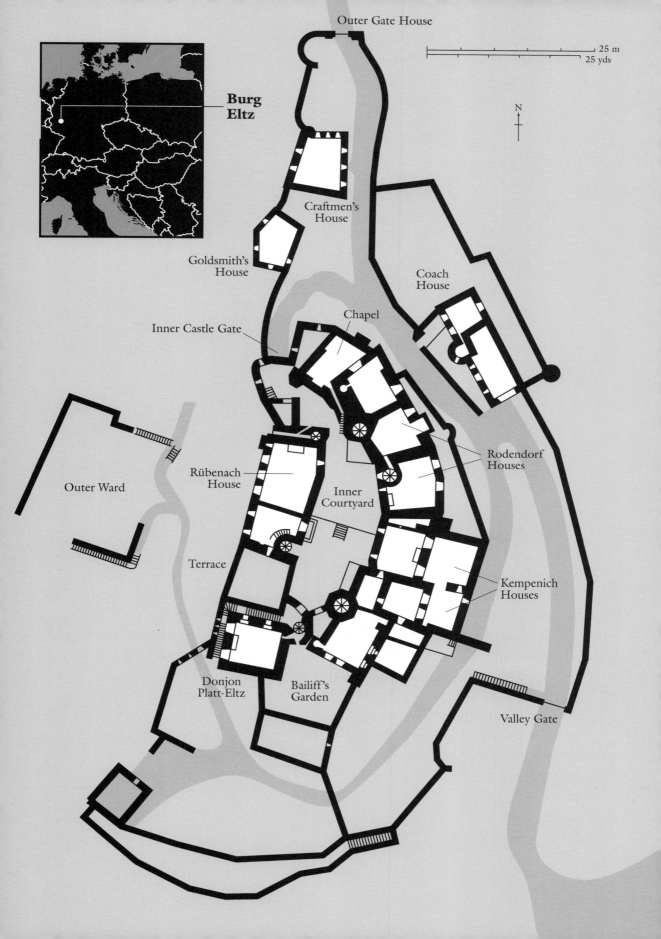

Outer Gate House

25 m
25 yds

N

Burg Eltz

Craftmen's House

Goldsmith's House

Coach House

Inner Castle Gate

Chapel

Rodendorf Houses

Rübenach House

Inner Courtyard

Outer Ward

Kempenich Houses

Terrace

Donjon Platt-Eltz

Bailiff's Garden

Valley Gate

LEFT: The iconic entrance to the medieval castle Burg Eltz.

RIGHT: One of many well preserved rooms featuring antique armoury.

at the time by hanging out with her warrior brothers, often engaging in mock battles with them. As was done at the time among such high aristocratic families, an arranged marriage was set up, when she was just a child, to the Knight of Braunsberg. Princess Agnes detested him and constantly ignored his attempts at courting. At a festive ball held at the castle, the knight grew tired of constant rebuffs by the princess, and decided to pull her onto the dance area and kiss her. Agnes, horrified, fought back and struck him across the face with a hard slap. He fled in indignation but the family feared repercussions for this incident, so they doubled the guards on duty for weeks. After time went by and nothing happened, the family let their guard down.

The rebuttal came in the form of the knight storming the castle with troops when the male members of the family were away on a three-day hunting trip. They killed the guardsmen and fought their way inside, destroying anyone in their path. Agnes, having spent her life sparring with her brothers, got into a breastplate of armour, one of her brother's helmets, and picked up a large battle-axe. The knight, failing to recognise Agnes in armour, fought back against what he presumed to be a family protector. Unfortunately, he delivered a fatal blow using a crossbow at close range, and when he removed her helmet he was shocked to find that it was Agnes all along. Both the ghost of Agnes and the Knight of Braunsberg have reportedly been seen on the grounds – Agnes pacing the doorway in her suit of armour, and the knight, a phantom horseman, roaming the grounds, begging for forgiveness for what he did. A different version of this legend says that the knight was locked inside the dungeon and now his ghost is trapped there, only released at nighttime where he roams the halls in eternal misery.

The Countess Room of the castle, which was Agnes' chambers, still holds the armour she died in and the battle-axe she fought with. This is said to be the most haunted part of the castle, where staff hear phantom whispering, voices, and see lights turn on and off. Some report locking up the castle at night only to return in the morning and find everything unlocked, nothing disturbed inside.

Dragsholm Castle

A baroque Danish building haunted by one hundred ghosts

Dragsholm Castle, known as *Dragholm Slot* in Danish, is a baroque-style castle about an hour's drive from Copenhagen, located on the island of Zealand. The name means 'the islet by the drag' and this was once the place where Vikings could drag their boats over in order to sail through to Roskilde without having to venture into the treacherous waters north of Zealand. It has a rich history and its impressive architecture makes it an appealing place to visit. It now functions as a hotel with a Michelin-starred restaurant attached to it. Beauty apart, one of its most famous 'facts' is that it's reportedly home to more than a hundred ghosts.

Originally built as a medieval palace in 1215 by a bishop, it was later fortified into a castle that became the only one to withstand the armies of Count Christopher during the Count's War that raged from 1534 to 1536 as part of the European Wars of Religion. This war brought about the Reformation of Denmark, which resulted in the castle, and all other Catholic belongings, being confiscated by the Crown. At this point, the Castle was turned into a prison – but this was no ordinary prison. It was for high ecclesiastical prisoners and grand nobility. It is some of these prisoners who are said to linger here today. One of the most famous ghosts and former prisoners here was James Hepburn, better known as Lord Bothwell, the third husband of Mary, Queen of Scots. Bothwell had been married to a Danish noblewoman at one time but had abandoned her and stolen the dowry her father had paid to him for their wedding. Controversially, he embedded himself in the court of Mary and, after murdering her husband, Lord Darnley, he later abducted the Queen and forced a marriage on her in order to become King Consort of Scotland. (Interestingly, later on, the remains of Lord Darnley were dug up and his skull was stolen.) Many people denounced this marriage and conflict ensued, which resulted in Bothwell escaping to Scandinavia. Unfortunately for him, he landed in the territory of his first wife. Her family had him imprisoned and he died at Dragsholm Castle in 1578 in truly appalling conditions. The pillar that he was chained to for the last years of his life can still be seen, with the circular groove still worn in the floor from his limited movements. His somewhat mummified remains can be found in a nearby chapel. Many believe that due to this horrendous death he is unable to rest and is bound to the grounds, where he has been seen

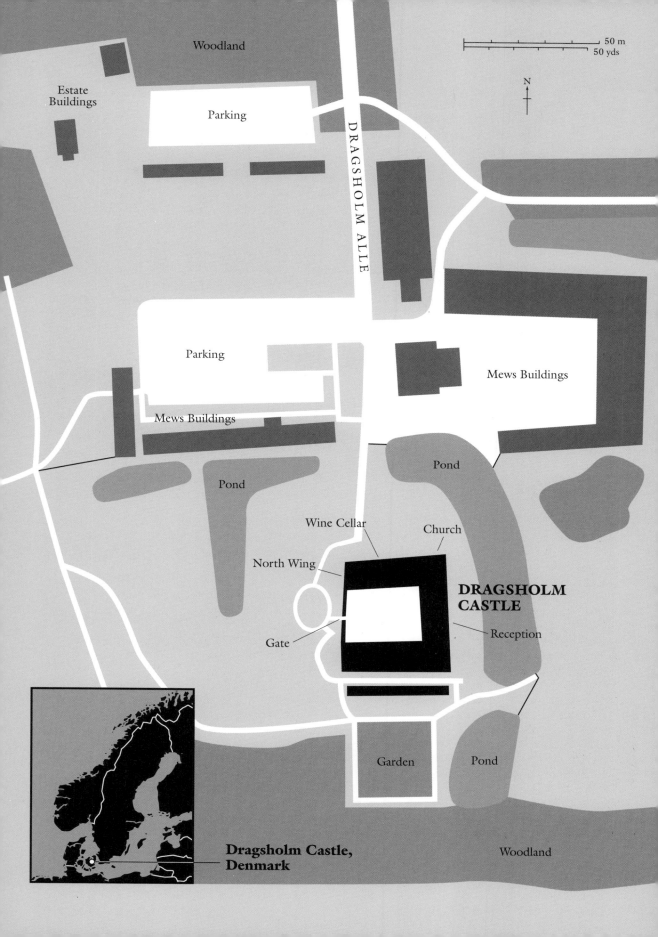

Woodland

Estate
Buildings

Parking

50 m
50 yds

N

D R A G S H O L M   A L L E

Mews Buildings

Parking

Mews Buildings

Pond

Pond

Wine Cellar

Church

North Wing

**DRAGSHOLM
CASTLE**

Gate

Reception

Garden

Pond

Woodland

**Dragsholm Castle,
Denmark**

riding a horse-drawn carriage and at other times on horseback. Some report hearing horses' hooves throughout the grounds, although no horses have been on the estate for many years.

Dragsholm also has a White Lady, which is a particular type of ghost best categorized as follows: female, appears wearing a white dress, is always mourning or crying, has died in connection to a lover (unrequited love, murdered by partner, jilted, unable to join partner in death, etc.). In this case, it is likely to be that of Celina Bolves, a well-to-do lady who fell in love with a commoner working at the castle. Against her family's wishes, she continued to see him and soon fell pregnant with his child, and when her father found out he had her imprisoned at the castle. There, she was chained to a wall and later bricked up inside part of the castle wall while still alive. Her screams and scratchings inside the wall can still be heard, with some reporting seeing a woman in a white dress sighing and roaming the halls in sorrow, looking for her lover. This legend was apparently confirmed in the 1930s when castle workers found a skeleton in a white dress walled up inside the castle, while doing repairs. It is difficult to verify this story, however, as it is said she was then buried in a nearby cemetery and a replica of her bones and dress were placed back into the hole with a pane of glass covering it so that visitors could see. It's possible that remains were indeed found but that the back story was retrofitted, or that the replica remains were simply added to bolster the White Lady story. This especially seems likely since the legend varies wildly and is sometimes attributed to one Celestine Mariann de Bayonne Gyldenstierne instead.

There is a happier female ghost on the grounds. This comes in the form of The Grey Lady. A Grey Lady is usually a female spirit who has died while unmarried and during a working task. They are often attributed to servants or nurses who have died on the grounds. In this castle it is believed that the Grey Lady was a young maid who worked there but did not live on the grounds. One day she was complaining of a terrible toothache and the lord of the castle took pity on her and offered her a poultice (a warm soft mass often spread with herbal medicine and applied to aches and pains). This relieved her toothache for a while and she went seeking the master of the house to thank him. Unfortunately, she was unable to do so and sometime in the next few days died, whether from infection or other means it is unclear. It is now said that she has returned to the castle, constantly looking to thank the man who helped her. She is seen as a positive, protecting and helpful force on the grounds. She is known to reward those who do good deeds and to look after guests and staff alike.

LEFT TOP: Dragsholm Castle, Zealand, Denmark.
LEFT BOTTOM: The apparently haunted 12th century medieval castle is now a famous restaurant and hotel.

The Han River

A river haunted by legendary water spirits

Seoul is not a place you might typically conflate with ghosts, although like any other long-standing city it has had its fair share of horror, violence and tragedy, but if you look close enough into the local legends some alarming stories start to emerge. The Han River is a place where many go for picnics on warm afternoons and take strolls along its banks at night. In fact, more than 50 per cent of the population voted it the most scenic place in all of Seoul, and has been central to the economic livelihood of Koreans for many years. It was also the site of many a gruesome tale and its victims are said to haunt the river. During a time when Korea was split into three factions vying for power, this river was used as the main trade route with China, via the Yellow Sea. The river is no longer used for trade or navigation and because its estuary is located right on the border with North Korea, it is barred from having any civilians use it.

Before it was reduced to a pretty landscape, the Han River is where several gruesome acts took place – and to this day, strange deaths occur in its waters. In 1866, during the Josean Dynasty, a large number of Catholics who were living in Korea, possibly as missionaries, were rounded up and brutally decapitated. Their heads were taken down to the Han River and rolled in en masse as a warning to a French military fleet that had arrived on the water, poised for invasion. The Josean Dynasty had a puritanical approach to what they believed Korea should be and this included a desire to eradicate all things considered 'foreign' – not just religious beliefs and cultural practices, but people too. If you were a foreign national or ex-pat living in Korea at the time, you would have great difficulty finding a grave to be buried in and eventually special cemeteries were built marked only for foreigners. This includes Yanghwajin Foreigners' Cemetery, built in 1890, which is actually close to the site of the Catholic beheading massacre; the initial beheadings took place at Jeoldusan, which translates roughly to 'Cut Head Mountain'.

Some go to this cemetery to pray for those who were murdered or treated mercilessly simply for being outsiders to the country. I have heard one lady say she brings offerings of rice and believes the ghosts linger on because she sees hand marks in the offerings she leaves out, believing that spirits come to take it. These offerings are more widespread than you may think; in a traditional memory ritual known as the *Jesa,* food and drinks are left out for

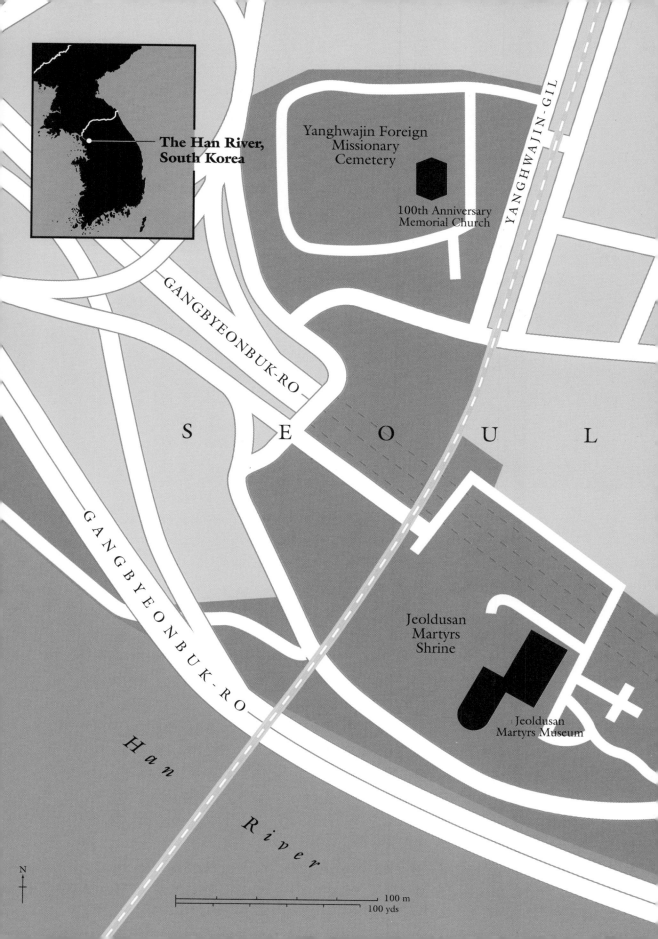

The Han River, South Korea

Yanghwajin Foreign
Missionary
Cemetery

100th Anniversary
Memorial Church

YANGHWAJIN-GIL

GANGBYEONBUK-RO

S   E   O   U   L

GANGBYEONBUK-RO

Jeoldusan
Martyrs
Shrine

Jeoldusan
Martyrs Museum

H a n

R i v e r

N

100 m
100 yds

the spirits of deceased relatives and ancestors every year on the anniversary of their passing. But it isn't just garden-variety ghosts believed to wander these places. The Han River has a particular type of supernatural entity known as the *Mul Gwishin* (물귀신).

This legendary type of ghost is believed to be the spirit of one who has drowned or died in water. The distinction made between a regular ghost, a creature and a *Gwishin* is that a ghost may be simply an ancestor (and therefore presumably helpful or non-threatening), a creature has a non-human or only part-human form, but a *Gwishin* is a type of ghost that is formed of a person unable to cross over because they harbour revenge or an uncompleted act. There are many different types but they usually have the core characteristics of appearing semi-transparent, being without legs, and are more commonly female. The female ones are often said to have long dark hair and wear a white Hanbok (a type of traditional funeral garment). These could be considered comparable to the type of ghost known as a White Lady in Western cultures.

The *Mul Gwishin* are unable to rest in their watery graves due to either committing suicide or being murdered. The ones connected to the Han River are often believed to be the souls of the decapitated Catholics, but newer ones have emerged in stories over the years, as bodies have been pulled from the river seemingly from having thrown themselves in or having died from inexplicable causes that seem to indicate foul play. The legends have additional physical characteristics in comparison to other *Gwishin* as they appear always to

be completely soaking wet and have extremely pale skin. There is also a belief that they have unnaturally long arms and if you get too close to one in the water it will pull you in and drown you. Perhaps most distressingly, it seems like these creatures are said to be able to appear in any body of water – including in bathtubs.

There is some hope to appease these vengeful spirits by making offerings and small sacrifices to them. The most notable of these takes place on Ganghwa Island every February – an island which has seen many massacres and violent confrontations since the Joseon Dynasty and is believed to be another concentrated place for these legendary water ghosts to reside. One of the reasons people believe so many of these spirits appear to be female is that women are said to hold more '*han*', which is a Korean concept that translates roughly to feelings of revenge or resentment towards past injustices, which makes them more likely to come back after death, seeking to appease these feelings. This is certainly reflected back in Korean pop culture, as most films dealing with supernatural concepts centre around female ghosts, monsters and hauntings. The Han River, in particular, made its way into pop culture in 2006 when a horror film called *The Host* was released, about a Korean family trying to save their daughter from a supernatural monster that emerges from the river.

ABOVE: Banpo Bridge illuminated at night over the Han River.

Chapter 5

Strange Nature

Gunnuhver

A volatile mud pool that trapped the spirit of an angry ghost

This area is a geothermal cap that has resulted in a tumultuous landscape of hot gas exploding from the ground, where shifts in Earth's tectonic plates have created fissures. Iceland as a whole is littered with volcanoes and constantly subject to earthquakes. This has given rise to attractive thermal springs, hot mud pools, and geysers that draw in many tourists, but the most famous of these springs, Gunnuhver, has its name and backstory rooted in a grim ghost story. Named for a local woman who starved to death 400 years ago, her spirit, according to their lore, has come back to murder her former landlord and his wife. A priest was called on to take care of the problem and solved it by casting said spirit into a boiling mud pool.

Gunnuhver is part of a rocky, barren landscape of green and blue rock, with its main opening just east of the oldest lighthouse in Iceland. It is the largest of all of Iceland's hot springs and is continuously spewing forth boiling hot steam at a temperature of almost 300°C (570°F) but the main feature of it is a bubbling mud pool measuring almost 66 feet (20 m) across that is known to be extremely volatile. In 2008, the entire area had to close for two years as the eruptions became so violent that they shot scalding hot mud and clay several feet in the air, subsequently destroying the former viewing platform, the wreckage of which can still be seen today. These geothermal areas are dangerous places to visit and caution should be exercised at all times.

The name Gunnuhver is taken from Guðrún, or *Gunna* for short, the name of a particularly angry female ghost. Gunnuhver essentially translates to 'Gunn's hot spring'. The legend of Gunna is documented in a collection of Icelandic folktales by Jón Árnason. In it he tells of the pitfalls of a man named Vilhjálmur Jónsson who lived at Kirkjuból (now known as Ísafjörður). Interestingly Kirkjuból was the site of the most famous witch trial in Iceland, which took place in 1656, and resulted in two men being burnt at the stake. Jónsson had a dispute with a woman named Guðrún Önundardóttir, who we know as Gunna. The disagreement was seemingly over a pot; this version implies it was part of a debt repayment, while other versions claim people were suspicious of Gunna because she was always brewing something in this pot. Either way, the conflict resulted in Gunna threatening and cursing him.

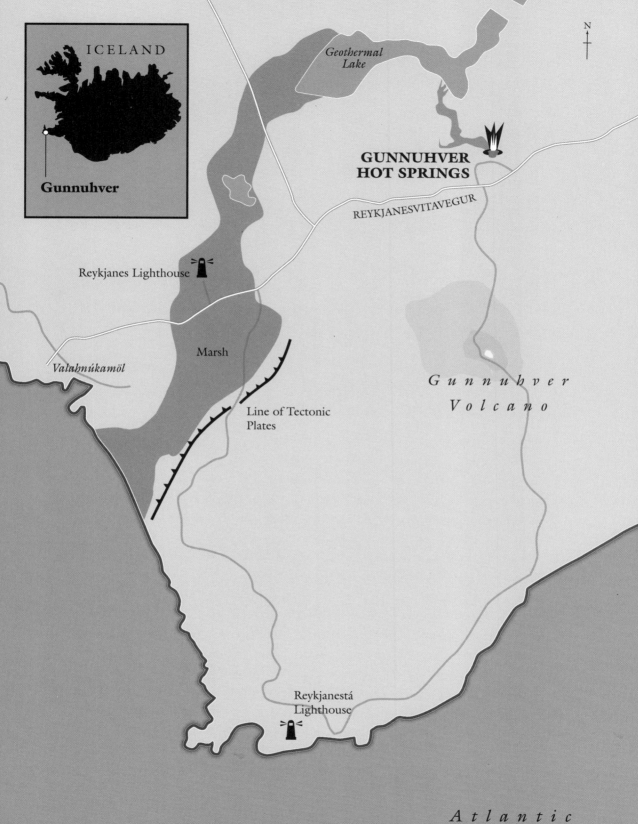

ICELAND

Gunnuhver

Geothermal Lake

N

GUNNUHVER HOT SPRINGS

REYKJANESVITAVEGUR

Reykjanes Lighthouse

Valahnúkamöl

Marsh

Line of Tectonic Plates

G u n n u h v e r
V o l c a n o

Reykjanestá Lighthouse

A t l a n t i c
O c e a n

500 m
500 yds

Shortly after this disagreement Gunna died and Jónsson turned up at her funeral while on his way to 'Skagi' (the colloquial name for the Reykjanes Peninsula – in Icelandic, its name is Reykjanesskagi). He never made it home and his body was found on the geothermal peninsula in a horrendous state of bruising and mutilation. The corpse was brought to the chapel at Kirkjuból where it was seen to by a minister, who was asked to stay with the body overnight as people feared it was Gunna who had done this to him, having risen from her grave in anger. The minister did so but endured a hellish night as he felt the body was constantly being pulled away from him by an unseen aggressive force. When Jónsson's widow died shortly after, this was also presumed to be the work of Gunna. It escalated and people wandering through the Skagi area began getting lost or losing their minds. She had now done so much damage that neither people nor animals could pass through. Fearing that she had grown too powerful, the local people hatched a plan to trap her.

They travelled to another minister and begged for his help, but he was known to be uncooperative without a drink and so, after plying him with alcohol, he finally agreed and his solution was to offer them a ball of wool. They were instructed to have Gunna grab hold of the loose end and allow the remaining ball to roll to a place where she could be trapped. The men returned and did as instructed – as soon as Gunna had hold of the string they let it roll and it eventually plunged into a mud pit at the hot springs. Gunna chased after it and found herself also plunged into the springs, after which no more harm came to the local people. Some believed that Gunna never let go of the string and that because it is so long, she is trapped over the edge of the pool and stuck there in perpetual torment.

The Gunna story is told slightly differently on a large sign near Gunnuhver. It says that Gunna was a local woman who failed to pay her rent to the crofter who owned the land she was on and as punishment he took away the only thing she owned of value – a cooking pot. She became enraged and after refusing to drink holy water she dropped dead. On the way to the cemetery, the men carrying her coffin noticed that it became increasingly lighter and they heard a voice saying 'no need deep to dig, no plans long to lie'. The next morning, they found the man who had taken her pot – he was dead and his corpse was blue with broken bones. The people of the peninsula became tormented and those who saw her ghost died. Some contacted a pastor, who was said to also be a sorcerer, and he gave them the ball of wool and instructions on how to trap her. Gunna followed it and she became stuck in the mud pool of the hot springs. This then became her home for the remainder of eternity. Those with 'second sight' have reported being able to still see her when looking over the edge. Some say if you listen closely, you can still hear Gunna's voice when the steam erupts.

LEFT: The Gunnuhver Geothermal area is connected to a legendary witch.
ABOVE: Gunnuhver Hot Springs blowing steam.

Aokigahara Forest

Japanese forest where hundreds of suicides take place

This strange and beautiful forest, also known as the 'sea of trees', lies on Honshu island in Japan, on the south west edge of Mount Fuji. It rests upon 11 square miles (30 sq km) of lava that poured down and cooled to form a hardened floor after the last major eruption of the Mount Fuji volcano in 864 CE. Lava rock is porous in nature and so creates many little pockets; this, in turn, absorbs a large volume of sound, contributing to the eerie stillness of the forest that some find unsettling. Many hikers come here and have to use coloured tape and rope in order not to become lost in the density of the forest, and there are also school trips brought here to explore the famous ice caves that form part of the region. But it isn't just the stillness or natural darkness here that unnerves visitors – the forest is a central place for *Yūrei*. This word is composed of two 'kanji'; the first being *Yū*, which means 'faint' or 'dim', and the second being *Rei*, which means 'spirit' or 'soul.' These *Yūrei* are a type of paranormal being that in Western cultures would be equivalent to a ghost.

There are several different types of *Yūrei* and they all have subtle differences from one another. The best way to understand them comes from analysing the etymology of their names. The correct usage of the word *Yūrei* is only when it denotes the spirit of a deceased human being, who has come back or is unable to pass on, but it is often used to describe a wider class of spirits in Japanese belief systems and mythology. One of the more complicated types is the *Yōkai*; although this word essentially means 'strange apparition' and is borrowed from the Chinese term *yaoguai*, used to describe monsters. The two kanji characters that compose the word both mean 'suspicious' or 'doubtful'.

The *Yōkai* are often portrayed in Western texts as demons but this is an incorrect simplification of their nature; they are, in fact, simply spirits that can come from both living and inanimate objects. Their nature can range from mischievous to malevolent and they take on many forms. Some examples would be the *Kappa*, which looks similar to a turtle, or the winged *Tengu*, a mixture of monkey features and human characteristics. The *Tengu*, in particular, is the most instantly recognizable, as its face, a red devil-like scowl with a long nose, is often carved onto masks. On a modern iPhone, you can find an emoji of this mask by typing the word 'Tengu' into your keyboard. They are one of several legendary

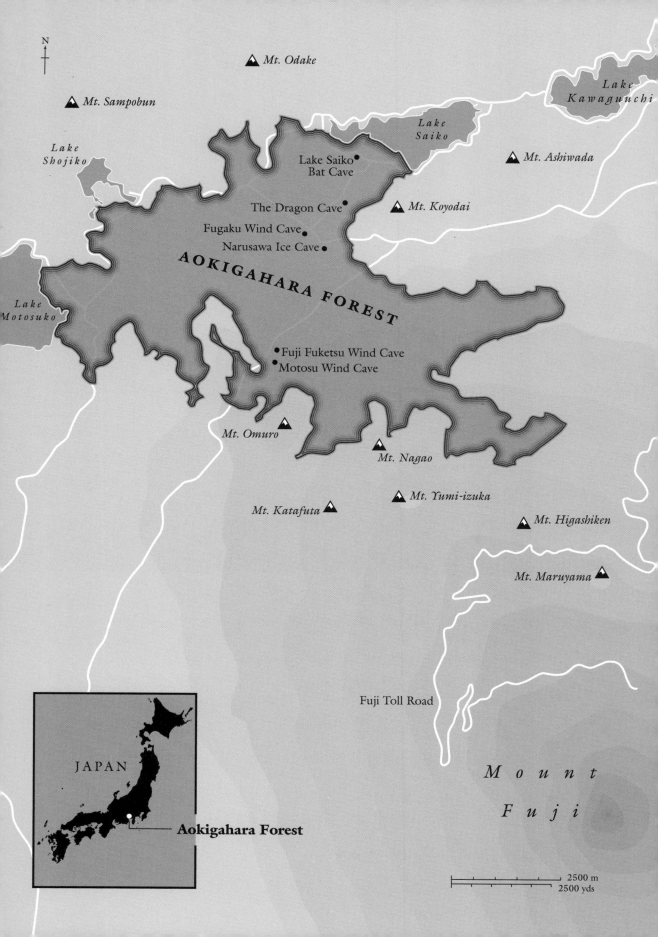

bird-type creatures within the Shinto religion, but in Buddhism they are classed as demons and harbingers of war. Some believe that this forest is home to one of them.

Yōkai can also come from non-living objects. This is because of a belief that all things, even objects and natural occurrences in nature, have vital consciousness or spirit to them. In the Middle Ages, in the Shinto religion, some believed that tools could have a type of spirit, especially if they had served for a long time. They became known as *Tsukumogami*.

Another class of *Yōkai* is the *Bakemono* – these are shape-shifters. Their true form may be that of an animal, but they take on the appearance of a human to terrorize the living. They may also take on more monstrous or creature-like forms. An example would be the *Noppera-bō,* which often impersonates the form of a familiar person, then its facial features dissolve to leave a completely blank face. Another example would be the *Uwan*, a grotesque creature with blackened teeth that can become a disembodied voice simply shouting the word 'Uwan!' repeatedly. They are said to dwell near old, abandoned buildings and temples. Some folklore states, that repeating the word back to them will make them flee.

Types of spirit can be split into two distinct categories: *Shiryō* and *Ikiryō*, the former being the spirits of the dead and the latter being the spirits of the living. The *Yūrei* are essentially the spirits of the dead who are unable to cross over into the afterlife. There are many reasons why this may happen but how it occurs is down to a person's soul (often referred to as one's '*reikon*') becoming altered and changing into a *Yūrei*. One of the chief causes for this being that a person did not receive any or the correct burial rites. Another reason may be that their death was sudden and/or violent, such as a murder or suicide, and that alters who they are. Some believe that such a violent death leaves them with too much emotion (desire for revenge, longing to stay on, unfinished business, sorrow, regret, etc.) and this somehow contorts the soul and they become this ghost-like entity.

A person who dies with a grudge or desire for revenge can become an O*nryō,* which is a type of *Yūrei* that is feared because it can cause harm to the living and even bring about natural disasters to enact its revenge. It is said that the lower social rank a person is, the stronger the *Yūrei* they may return as, which is grounded in believing that they will have been treated more harshly in their life than that of someone born in a higher class. This classification system showing that not all ghosts and creatures are equal also coincides partly with some of the beliefs about how a *Tengu* comes to be. Texts written in the late Kamakura period (1185–1333) say that the *Tengu* are souls who have fallen onto this path due to excessive pride; they cannot go to 'hell' because they do not have the right belief systems but cannot go to 'heaven' because they were bad people. It also states that a knowledgeable person can become a *Daitengu* (Greater Tengu) and an ignorant one would become *Kotengu* (Small Tengu). The *Daitengu,* in particular, are connected with sacred forests and mountains. Mount Fuji, overlooking the Aokigahara Forest, is connected to a *Daitengu* known as *Daranibō.*

The Aokigahara Forest is believed to be home to so many *Yūrei* due to the high number of suicides committed within its realm. It has come to be known as the 'suicide forest' and there are now markers on the trails urging people not to take their own lives and to contact suicide helplines. At the entrance a sign says, 'life is a precious thing that you get from your parents'. In 2003, there were more than 105 suicides committed here; by 2010, the police had reported more than 240 suicide attempts, with 54 of them being completed. Annual body searches have been conducted by the police and volunteers here since the 1970s. The rate is so bad that the police have now stopped publicizing the numbers in an attempt to decrease the association between the forest and suicide, but Japan has a high rate of suicide all over. In 2022, according to website Mental Floss, suicide rates increased worldwide by 2.7 per cent, making it a leading cause of death for women between the ages of 15 and 34, and men aged between 20 and 44. There is mass speculation as to why people favour this place to take their own lives, with some attributing it to the novel *Kuroi Jukai* written by Matsumoto, who helped popularize detective fiction in Japan. In the book, the two lovers go to this forest to take their own lives together. But this novel was published in 1960 and the history of death and suicide in the forest predates it.

Suicide in most cultures is seen as an act of shame or desperation, but in Japan its history is sometimes linked with dying honourably. In feudal-era Japan, Samurai warriors would die by suicide, sometimes in an act of ceremonial disembowelling, rather than be captured by an enemy. Even much later, in the Second World War, a special class of soldiers known as the Kamikaze flew suicide missions. But death perceived as being less than honourable is often hidden, and this dense and hushed forest provides that space. Scholars have been arguing for years whether suicide was ever particularly common previously in Japanese culture, and it is hard to separate fact from folklore.

One of the earliest stories to emerge about this forest was that during feudal times food was scarce and so some families would take an older relative who was depending on them for food and care, or who was deemed ill, to the forest, where they would be abandoned. This act was known as *ubasute*. Through poetry and folklore this act became entangled with the forest and many believed that the *Yūrei*, who haunted the forest, were the spirits of the old ones who had been left to die by their families. It is hard to pinpoint exactly when the forest became a hotspot for suicide, but we do know that hikers and visitors were finding bodies as early as the 1950s.

It isn't just bodies that turn up but also moss-covered shoes, abandoned clothing, purses and briefcases, final notes and other personal belongings. It is increasingly difficult to estimate how many have died here because bodies are consumed by the forest as roots and plants grow over the remains. Bodies will also be picked apart by animals, causing bones and flesh to be scattered across a large area or stolen away into animal dens. March has been charted as the time of year when the suicides spike in the forest and it is believed that this is because it is the end of the fiscal year in Japan. With so much pressure on people to be successful and work hard it may have a counter effect of leading people to desperation and death. And it isn't just local people who come here to take their own lives – between 2013 and 2015 alone it was found that more than one hundred of the bodies recovered from here were those of people who did not come from the surrounding and nearby regions.

Visitors have noted that compasses do not work properly here, and although this is repeatedly attributed to paranormal phenomena (because in paranormal investigations two things that are affected the most are electrical equipment and magnetic equipment), there's likely a more natural explanation. Because the floor of the forest is made of cooled lava, it will have a high concentration of iron in its make up; if a compass is placed down on the floor its magnetism will be affected by the iron, causing it to give strange readings.

The combination of eerie stillness due to the forest's high absorption of sound, the perpetual darkness due to the thickness of the tree pattern and it being an area heavily connected to tragic death, all lend itself to the supernatural. Of course, some come to visit the area searching for these gruesome deaths, an act we now often refer to as 'dark tourism'. One of the most infamous examples of this is the YouTube personality Logan Paul who travelled there in 2018 and filmed himself discovering the remains of a person who had taken their own life. The video caused a massive backlash, rightfully so, and stands as a reminder that just because other people might find shocking discoveries sensationalist, it doesn't make it morally right. If you do travel to the forest, either for its sprawling natural beauty or out of an interest in Japanese folklore, do bear in mind that it is also a site of great tragedy and grief. Stay on the paths and respect the forest.

PREVIOUS LEFT: The eerie Aokigahara Forest of Japan.
PREVIOUS RIGHT: 155 Depiction of a Yūrei.
NEXT: A single shoe remains at the scene of an apparent suicide in Aokigahara forest.

Door To Hell

Massive desert crater that has been burning for decades

Turkmenistan is a remote, landlocked country in Central Asia and second-largest in the region. Most of it is covered by the Karakum Desert and it possesses the fifth-largest reserves of natural gas in the world. Darvaza (known as *Derweze* in the native Turkmen language) is one of its most rural counties, located in the middle of the desert, and is primarily home to the Teke tribe, who continue to live a nomadic lifestyle. In this barren landscape is a large crater of unending burning fire known as the 'door to hell'.

Stretching an impressive 230 feet (70 m) across and approximately 100 feet (30 m) deep, this gigantic crater has become both a wonder to committed tourists and geologists alike. The crater produces no smoke but is filled with hundreds of small fires that have been burning for decades. This gives it a perpetually illuminated and hellish appearance, resulting in its nickname. Known in the Turkmen language as '*Garagum ýalkymy*', meaning 'the shining of Karakum', this natural wonder has been the focus of much debate regarding its origins. Many documents that may help us understand how the continually burning gas crater began are either missing or classified, but local geologists have stated that they believe it began in the 1960s when the hole collapsed into the large crater it is now, but that the burning only began in the 1980s and that this was done initially to prevent potentially poisonous gases from being released. If part of the ground collapses in a natural gas field, such as this one, it would be set on fire in order to burn off the gas until the source runs out; the problem is that if the volume of gas is severely underestimated then what one gets is a continually burning emission. Consider the difference between lighting a short burst of gas from an aerosol can versus lighting the gas ring of a stove.

Others believe that the 'door to hell' began in the early 1970s when a Soviet operation drilling there for oil accidentally collapsed due to the structural weakness of the ground. They then attempted to 'flare' the area, an act that is common in oil drilling operations to eliminate excess gas, and unfortunately the 'excess' gas was continuous gas being released from the earth. It isn't just the heat or hellish appearance that is frightening; the Canadian explorer George Kourounis was the first man to be sent down into the 'door to hell' just a few years ago in order to take samples of the soil at the bottom (to better understand if life can survive under such harsh conditions), and he describes the noise of the flames as being 'jet engine like'.

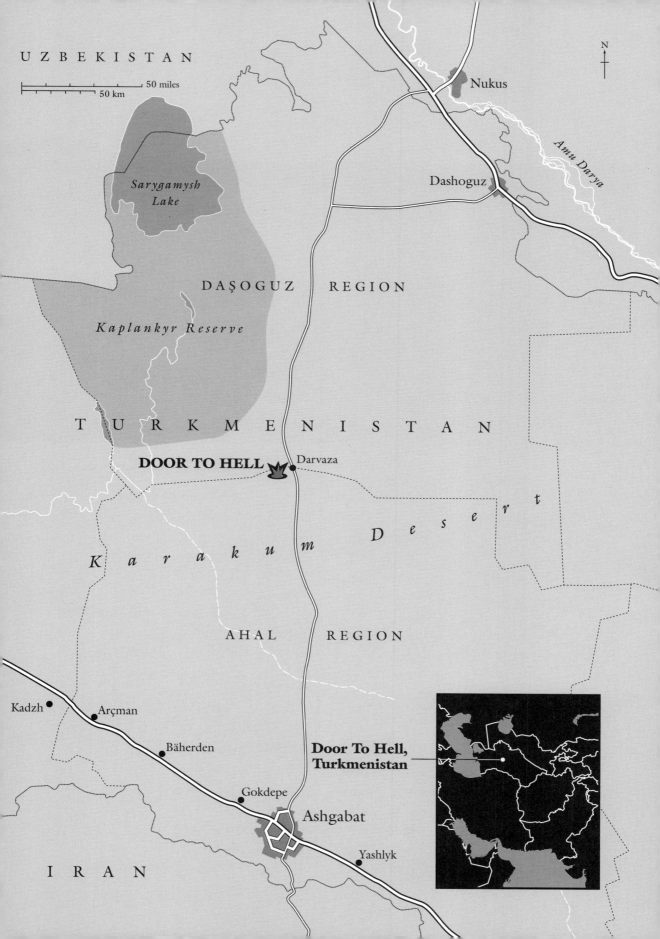

UZBEKISTAN

50 miles
50 km

Sarygamysh
Lake

DAŞOGUZ   REGION

Kaplankyr Reserve

Nukus

Amu Darya

Dashoguz

T U R K M E N I S T A N

DOOR TO HELL ☼ • Darvaza

K   a   r   a   k   u   m   D   e   s   e   r   t

AHAL   REGION

Kadzh •

Arçman •

Bäherden •

Gokdepe •

Ashgabat

Yashlyk •

**Door To Hell,
Turkmenistan**

I R A N

N

Naming landmarks as entrance points to hell isn't uncommon and it creates an interesting intersection between what hell actually means to people of different faiths, why we consider it to be associated with fire, and why these places are naturally positioned downwards into the earth. Turkmenistan is predominantly Muslim (more than 90 per cent of the population), with a small portion being Christian (around 5 per cent). In the Islamic faith, 'hell' is known as Jahannam. This is the place in the afterlife where people go to be punished physically and psychologically for their sins or lack of faith. Jahannam is essentially built up of layers or levels. In the Qur'an, this hell is described as having seven gates or entrances, but the ideology of hell as a multi-level plain predates that.

Before the Qur'an there were short reports and scripts of the Prophet Muhammad called 'Hadiths'. Here, the Islamic hell is discussed in much more elaborate detail, most notably saying that it has seven levels, that it is enormous (so deep that if you threw a stone into it, it would take seventy-years for it to hit the bottom), and that it has 70,000 valleys, each containing 70,000 scorpions and serpents. Although several types of punishment are described here, it wasn't really until the twelfth century that specific levels were assigned to specific types of sinners – this was done largely by the scholar Qadi Ayyad. This eschatological structuring went on to influence many notable literary works about hell, namely *Inferno* by Dante Alighieri, who all but lifted the entire structure for his famous depiction of hell, right down to the very furthest depth being not hot but rather a barren, icy tundra. The Hadiths also introduce us to the link between religious punishment and fire in the Islamic faith. In one, the prophet is quoted as saying, 'Fire of the children of Adam,

LEFT: The Darvaza Crater blazes with perpetual flame.

ABOVE: The gas crater is known as 'The Door to Hell' due to it's ominous appearance at night.

which they kindle, is a seventieth part of the fire of Jahannam'. The 'children of Adam' here are the humans and the fires are 'as black as tar'. We can also see the connection between the belief of hell as a physical place, it being composed of fire, and it being beneath the surface of the earth in these early scriptures. This then influenced the seven names used in the Qur'an to describe hell, with Jahannam only being the first layer. Beneath that you have *al-Laza* (the blaze), then *al-Hutama* (the consuming fire) and so on, until you reach the seventh level, *al-Hawiya*, which is simply an abyss. With this in mind, it makes sense why a large pit burning in endless fire in the middle of the desert then might be known as 'the door to hell'.

Several Islamic scholars have tried to work out where the physical entrance to this fiery afterlife could be; some believed that the sea was in fact the top level, while others said that the doorway is in Yemen in the form of a well, poisoned with sulphur, which is haunted by damned souls. Many talk about the Valley of Hinnom as being the definitive entrance way to hellfire, since, in the ancient Hebrew Bible it was the place where *tophet* was conducted. This was a ritual sacrifice to the god Moloch that required children to be killed with fire. The valley became referred to as Gehinnom (גֵּיהִנֹּם) in Hebrew, which survived into ancient Aramaic and became a word synonymous with both hell and purgatory in Christian texts and later religions. If anyone wants to test this particular entrance point in Turkmenistan, then they perhaps should do so now: the government there has ordered that the hellfire pit be extinguished in the next year or so.

Lake Maracaibo

36-million-year-old lake with perpetual thunderstorm

This ancient vase-shaped lake is located in north western Venezuela and covers an area of 5,217 square miles (about 13,512 sq km), making it the largest lake in all of South America. It's also one of the oldest lakes on Earth, having been formed approximately 36 million years ago. More than a quarter of the population of Venezuela live around the edges of this lake, forming neighbourhoods of multi-coloured houses on stilts perched in the water – with boats used as the main source of transport between these floating villages. The main body of water that feeds this lake is the Catatumbo River, along the basin of which live the indigenous Bari people, and it is from these people's language that the word '*Catatumbo*' emerges – meaning 'house of thunder'. The area is known as such because it is home to the highest density of lightning in the world.

The specific atmospheric phenomenon known as 'Catatumbo lightning' occurs primarily over the mouth of this great lake, at the point where the river pours in and creates a bog-like area. The actual mechanism of how this mega-storm occurs is thought to be because winds are constantly blowing across the open lake and swamp plains, picking up heat and moisture that create electrical charges, but when they hit the three mountain ranges that enclose the area – the Andes, Perija and Merida's Cordillera – the air is destabilized, resulting in mass thunderstorm activity. This phenomenon has been called the 'Lanterns of Saint Anthony' and the 'Lighthouse of Maracaibo'; this latter phrase was used by many explorers here, as the continuous lightning meant that those on boats had their navigational equipment constantly illuminated and could sail towards the mouth of the lake using the storm as a sort of lighthouse or beacon.

To give you an idea of exactly how much lightning is produced here, it occurs on an average of 297 nights a year, for an average of 9 hours per day, and there can be anywhere from 16 to 40 lightning flashes per minute. At its peak season in September, the area can experience up to 280 lightning strikes per hour. Using NASA observation systems, researchers have worked out that this area has an average of 250 instances of lightning per square kilometre.

How the lake itself came to be formed is told in an Indigenous folktale featuring more supernatural beings. It is said that the area was once covered with rainforest and was ruled

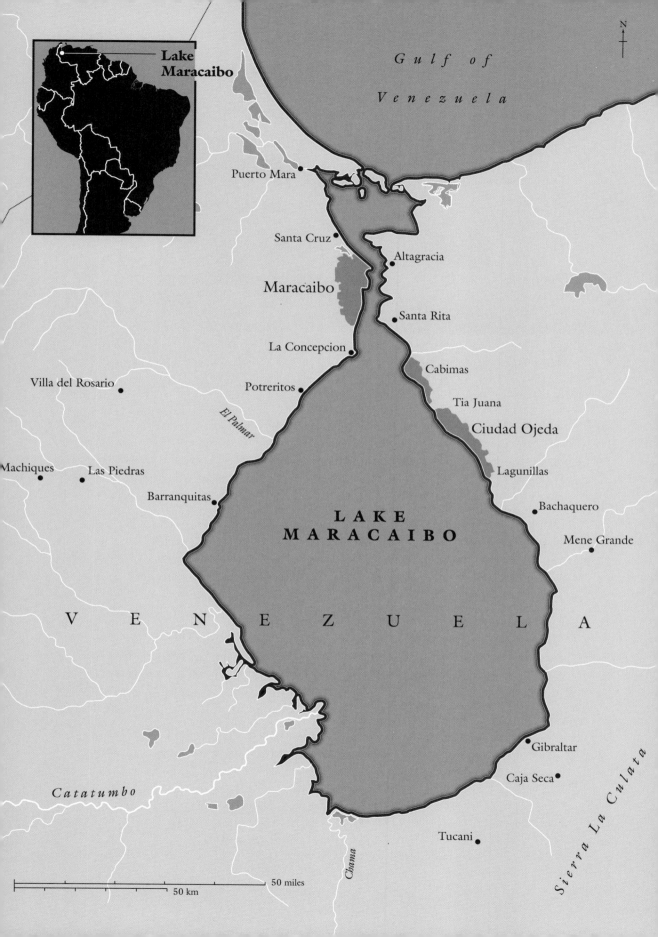

Lake
Maracaibo

Gulf of

V e n e z u e l a

N

Puerto Mara

Santa Cruz

Altagracia

Maracaibo

Santa Rita

La Concepcion

Cabimas

Potreritos

Tia Juana

Villa del Rosario

Ciudad Ojeda

El Palmar

Lagunillas

Machiques

Las Piedras

Bachaquero

Barranquitas

Mene Grande

**L A K E
M A R A C A I B O**

V E N E Z U E L A

Gibraltar

Caja Seca

Catatumbo

Sierra La Culata

Tucani

Chama

50 miles

50 km

by a leader known as The Great Zápara (Zápara/Sápara is also the name of an endangered Indigenous rainforest tribe whose last remaining members now reside in nearby Peru and Ecuador). He instructed his people to build villages on the outskirts of the forest and planned to keep the rainforest for himself, at the heart of which he erected a large palace using only the sound of his voice. There he lived with his daughter, Maruma, who was a great poet and singer. He forbade Maruma from marrying as he wanted to keep her poetry and singing all to himself. One day he left the palace on a trip and his daughter went out into the forest on a hunt for game. She came across an animal that had been shot down with another person's arrows. Furious that a person had ventured into the sacred forest that was supposed to be reserved only for her royal family, she confronted them.

The other hunter was a young man, Tamare. He justified his hunt, telling her that he had been expelled from his village for not being useful enough – his only true skill was that of poetry and song. Maruma was intrigued to meet another poet and invited him back to the palace where they feasted to celebrate the hunt and gave themselves over to long hours of songs and verses. As time passed around them, Zápara eventually returned, and, upon hearing the voice of his daughter entangled with the voice of a man, he flew into a rage. He stamped his feet on the ground so hard that the forest began to sink into a large basin, the mighty rivers of the surrounding mountain ranges began to pour into this and with his supernatural powers he commanded the land to the north to open, resulting in the sea crashing into this great abyss. Zápara then handed his ruling powers to his son, Maracaibo, and threw his body into the water where he became an island. The lovers continued their songs oblivious to the rising water filing the palace and eventually drowned, the water bringing the waves of their final requiem to the surface. Now, the lake does not cry out like the sea or laugh as other lakes do, but rather it whispers poetry and sings songs of infinite love.

ABOVE: View of Ologa, a small village made of stilt houses in Maracaibo Lake.
RIGHT: This lake sees the highest density of lightning in the world.

Dumas Beach

Black sand beach that may have been coloured by burnt bodies

Dumas Beach is a rural spot, located in the southern portion of the state of Gujarat on the west coast of India. Bordering the Arabian Sea, it is popular among tourists and one of its most striking features is its black sand. A beach may have black sand for one of two natural reasons: first, that it is near a volcano and when lava hits the water and cools, it shatters into tiny black fragments called basalt that can form black sand beaches virtually overnight: second, it can be the result of 'placer deposits' – when valuable minerals are separated from other sediment by gravity and part of the process results in a heavy and partially magnetic black sand. These placer deposits were what started the gold rushes in America and diamond mines in Africa.

There's also a third explanation for the black sand, one rooted in folklore and local supernatural legend. It is said that the beach was once used as a cremation ground for Hindus, and that so many people were burnt here that the ash mixed with the natural sand, resulting in its dark appearance. It is also why many believe the beach is haunted. People reportedly hear sounds coming from the beach at night when it is empty, both laughter and crying, and it is said that some of those who stay after dark go missing. There is even a report of a man being found dead here with his tongue hanging out of his skull. Other stories include strange lights, dogs acting aggressively and howling constantly when taken near the beach at night and white apparitions that seem to roam aimlessly upon the black sands.

Why would this beach be a Hindu cremation ground? Hindus have sixteen sacraments known as *Sanskars,* the first of which takes place before a person's birth and the last occurs after death. In order to reach the afterlife the soul of a Hindu is required to cross over a river of blood; how difficult this task will be is determined by a person's good deeds (*punya*) and bad deeds (*paap*) in life.

To help this soul begin its journey, Hindu death rites are a series of rituals, as opposed to one ceremony, as you would see in Christian funerals. Fire is always present in Hindu ceremonies, from weddings to small rituals at home, and the funeral is perhaps the most important of them all. A large open air pyre is used for traditional Hindu funerals and the importance of the act lies in the belief that a person must be burnt in order to separate the

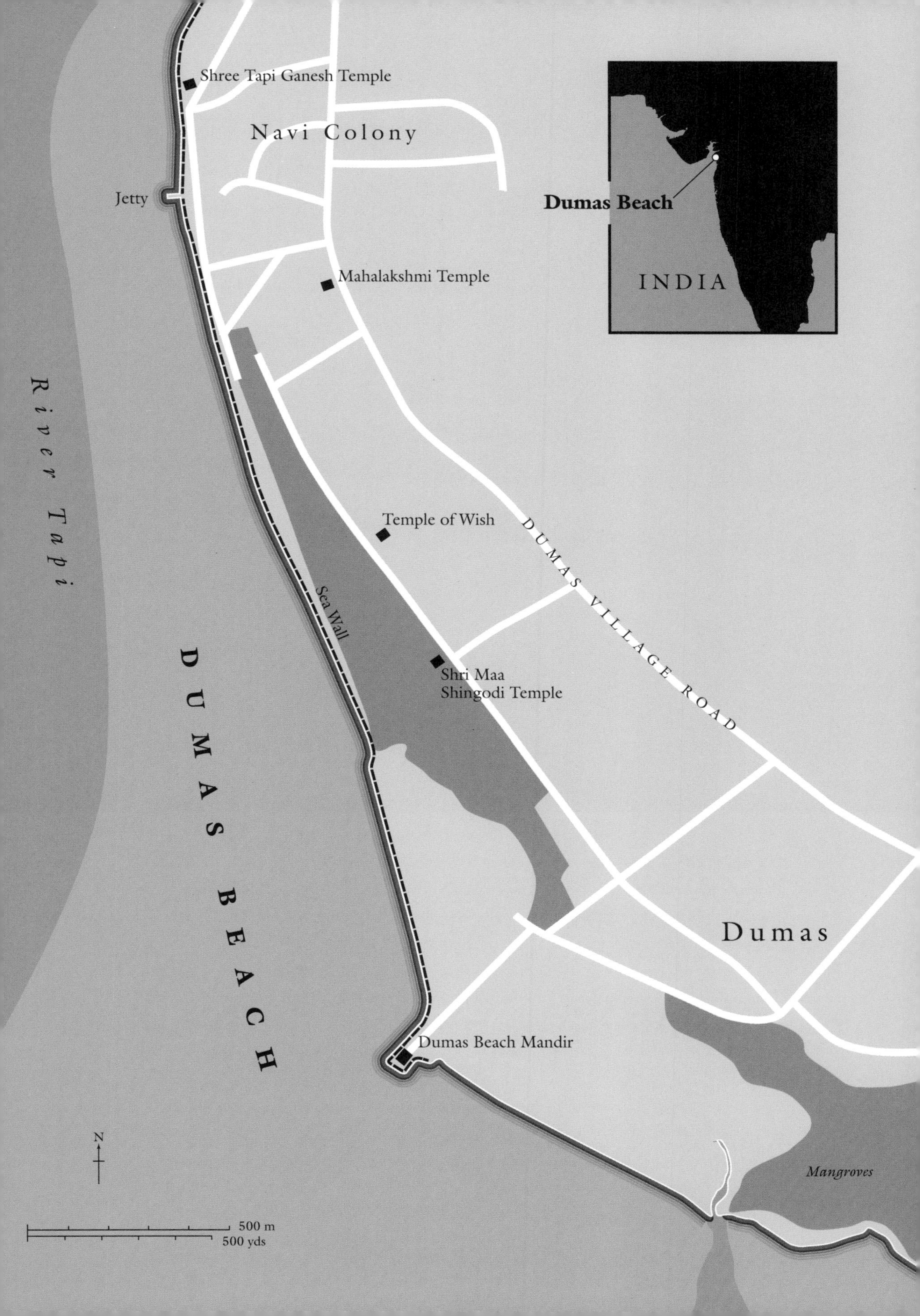

Shree Tapi Ganesh Temple

Navi Colony

Jetty

Mahalakshmi Temple

River Tapi

Sea Wall

Temple of Wish

DUMAS VILLAGE ROAD

Shri Maa
Shingodi Temple

D U M A S   B E A C H

Dumas

Dumas Beach Mandir

N

Mangroves

500 m
500 yds

Dumas Beach

INDIA

soul from the physical body so it can begin its journey. So, if this is a site where correct burial rites have been observed, why would it be haunted? Surely the dead have passed on to whatever the next realm is, aided by their rituals, and have no motive to return. Or is it that all places connected with death have the propensity to be haunted?

The difficulty here is in verifying the history of the beach. It's not uncommon for Hindu cremation ceremonies to take place near bodies of water – traditionally, many people are burnt along the Ganges River in a month-long funeral ceremony. But in contrast to a river the beach would have a constant tide coming in and out that would make it a difficult place to conduct this. Even if there was a truly staggering amount of ash here from many remains, it is unlikely it would form black sand, as ash would simply be washed away or dissolved by the tide. There would likely be large amounts of dark staining on the beach for a temporary period of time and the constant heat from the burnings would definitely alter the sand, but the sheer volume and size of the beach makes it unlikely that that is what occurred here. Regardless, it is possible to see the effect of these beliefs on both locals and tourists alike.

When the sun sets, the police begin clearing the beach and it remains empty at night; a derelict eeriness falls and people avoid the area.

While whole shoals of fish have washed up dead on the beach and the corpse of a fully grown forest deer covered in bite marks was found here by locals in April 2023, there are probable explanations for these phenomena. Belief that this beach is haunted remains strong among visitors, perhaps resulting in people having strange or inexplicable experiences. These may be a result of priming effects (you know you are in an area with haunted lore) that cause people to attribute normal phenomena to supernatural means, and the results of fear negating the brains cognitive processes, especially at night. People themselves are sometimes at risk of generating their own haunting through the indomitable power of folklore.

ABOVE: Sunset over the black sands of the Dumas Beach, Gujarat, India.

Skinwalker Ranch

American ranch home to many UFO and monster sightings

This controversial large ranch of more than 500 acres (about 2 kilometres) was previously known as Sherman Ranch and is located in Uintah County, Utah, USA. Over several decades it has been a high-density site for UFO reports, poltergeist activity, paranormal phenomena and folklore-related horror. UFO reports in newspapers from this area begin around 1970 and the first time this ranch appears connected to them in the newspapers is around 1996. However, the ranch had been nicknamed 'UFO Ranch' as far back as the 1950s due to the constant phenomena experienced there. The ranch backs onto the Uintah and Ouray Indian Reservation, home to many people of the Ute tribe. Its current name, Skinwalker, in fact refers to a creature from Native American beliefs, one that primarily resides among the Navajo, or Diné, people.

There are actually several different varieties of these creatures but the one most people would be familiar with is what in the Navajo language is known as '*Yee Naaldlooshii*', which roughly means '*it goes on all fours*'. These creatures are believed to be witches practising dark magic, who are able to transform into, or possess, the bodies of animals, usually deformed ones that are connected to particular omens – such as the coyote or wolf. The issue with trying to conceptualize folklore from Native American beliefs is that external cultures lack the framework to understand these in the same way as they are understood in their Indigenous belief systems – there is also great difficulty with people taking these stories and warping them into Western narratives. You'll find that Navajo or Diné people very rarely ever discuss skin-walkers with outsiders. But they aren't the only ones with this creature in their belief systems – types of skin-walkers appear in the legends of the Apache, Pueblo and Hopi people, too.

Terry and Gwen Sherman, the previous owners of the ranch, had many experiences while living there. They had a run-in with a wolf described to be three times average size, which survived multiple gunshots being fired into it. They reported several cattle simply vanishing; some would have tracks in the snow that would simply stop, while some were found mutilated (a hole cut into the centre of the eye, or the rectum removed); others were found dead in a clump of trees with all the branches above it seemingly cut off. Terry said he would hear voices while out walking his dog; they spoke a language he couldn't understand,

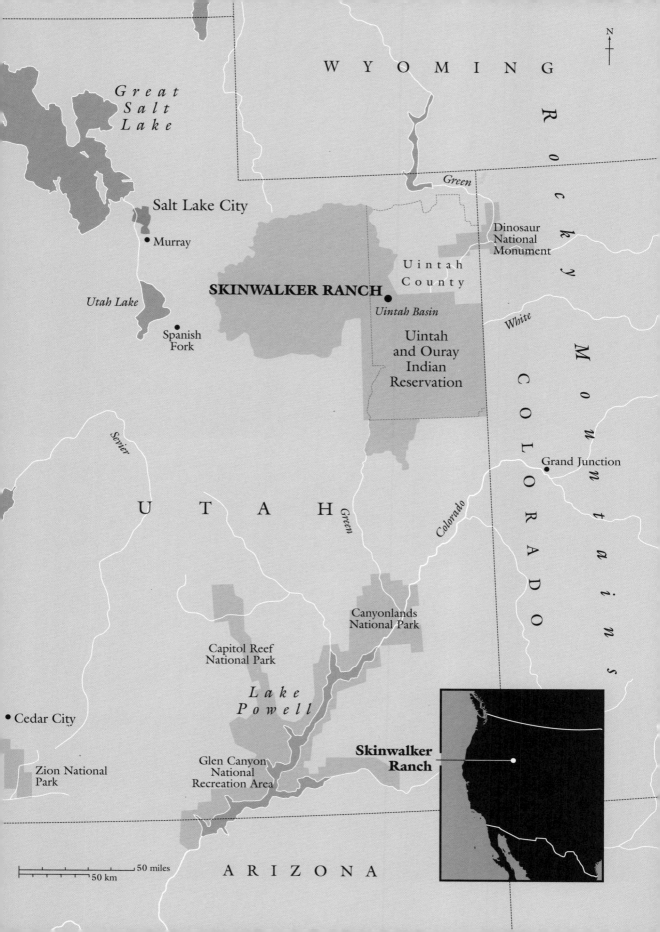

seeming to come from about 25 feet (about 7.6 m) away, but there was nothing there, and they caused his dog to go berserk. According to locals, since the 1950s, there have been reports of UFO-related activity – strange lights, craft that didn't match any known aircraft, and crop circles. The Shermans only stayed for two years and afterwards the ranch was bought by millionaire Robert Bigelow, the founder of NIDSci (National Institute for Discovery Science).

Bigelow wanted to use the place to study paranormal and UFO phenomena. During this time many people investigated here, with a variety of experiences totalling more than one hundred recorded inexplicable or seemingly supernatural incidents. Four core people who had experiences there were: retired US Army Colonel John B. Alexander, Colm Kelleher and his co-author George Knapp, and the Defence Intelligence Agency official James Lacatski. Alexander had been an advocate for the integration of paranormal studies into defence programmes during his army career – with a strong interest in UFO phenomena he put together a group of government officials with high security clearance to ascertain whether or not the government had been concealing the knowledge and application of alien technology. Kelleher and Knapp published a book about the ranch titled *Hunt for the Skinwalker* in 2005; this was subsequently read by DIA official Lacatski, who reached out to visit the ranch. There, Lacatski had an experience that could be described as supernatural and, once it was relayed to several senators, they all agreed that a large portion of money from the Department of Defence budget should be allocated to studying the anomalous phenomena that was taking place there – $22 million, to be exact.

The goal was to use current, independent and empirical scientific methodology to explore the variety of goings-on. Audio visual recordings, measuring equipment, night vision, security alerts and more were all employed. Although more than one hundred instances of unexplained phenomena were reported over the years there was no proof given that was rigorous enough to be accepted by an empirical peer-reviewed scientific journal. The theories of why this place endures so much strange horror vary, but a prominent theory is that when the land originally belonged to the Indigenous Ute people, they got into a dispute with Navajo people, who released or conjured skin-walkers on their behalf. There are stories that Ute people will not cross this land because they consider it the path of the skin-walker, but the hesitancy to speak about it among local tribes makes it impossible to verify their beliefs. Other ideas are that it's all UFO connected, that the area is constantly visited and modified by something not from this planet. Another is that the Shermans made it all up to sell their land to Bigelow. Of course, there's no way to prove this, but the area had lots of strange reports for decades before the Shermans ever lived there and they only sold the place for US$200,000, which is a low price for such a ranch, and, at the time was the same cost of a basic family home.

LEFT TOP: An image photographed by Christopher Bartel during his time working at Skinwalker Ranch in Utah's Uinta Basin.
LEFT BOTTOM: A skull of a dead cow killed in the forest lies on the ground.

San Clemente

The unofficial UFO capital of the world

This Andean mountain city and commune in the Maule Region of Chile has a population of 40,000, with most people living in rural areas. It is a place of spectacular beauty, with rocky wildlife preserves, waterfalls and lagoons. But it isn't just the natural attractions that lead most people here, but rather the supernatural strangeness – San Clemente is considered the unofficial UFO capital of the world.

Reports of unidentified craft in the sky, unearthly lights and unsettling encounters started to emerge in newspapers around 1995 – but it wasn't just your usual UFO sightings. In San Clemente there's shining spheres that disappear into the woodland and into bodies of water. Since then, hundreds more inexplicable cases have come from the area, at an estimated average of one report per week. It was happening so often that in 2008 the government set up a 'UFO trail' that maps out where the main hotspots are. This trail is 19 miles (30 km) long and takes you through the Andean mountains and forest ranges, including Colbún Lake, which is believed to attract so many UFOs because of its high mineral quality.

Lakes come up frequently when looking at maps of UFO sightings. There's a variety of theories as to why this may be, but the most prominent ones among researchers is that if life not from this planet were to visit, they may either be interested in taking samples of, or examining, our life sources (such as large bodies of water) or may actually require the components of such places (minerals, chemicals, basic elements), for whatever reason. These places have many confounding factors in any supernatural occurrences because there are simply so many things that can affect what we experience here; for example, the water altering our perception of light sources, reflections creating bounce-back, sound behaving strangely due to the open area or echoes behaving in a way that confuses our senses, etc.

Another hotspot on this trail is El Enladrillado. This elevated site sits at 7,217 feet (2,200 m) above sea level and is one of the world's top fifty largest stone megaliths that remain today. It requires a four-hour long horseback ride to get there, but it's a pilgrimage very much worth making to those interested in ancient stone structures, UFO sites and the wonders of the old world. The megalith is composed of a staggering 233 gigantic rectangular stones, with some as big as 16 feet (4.8 m) wide and 30 feet (9 m) long, arranged in an amphitheatre-like formation. It feels like the Chilean version of The

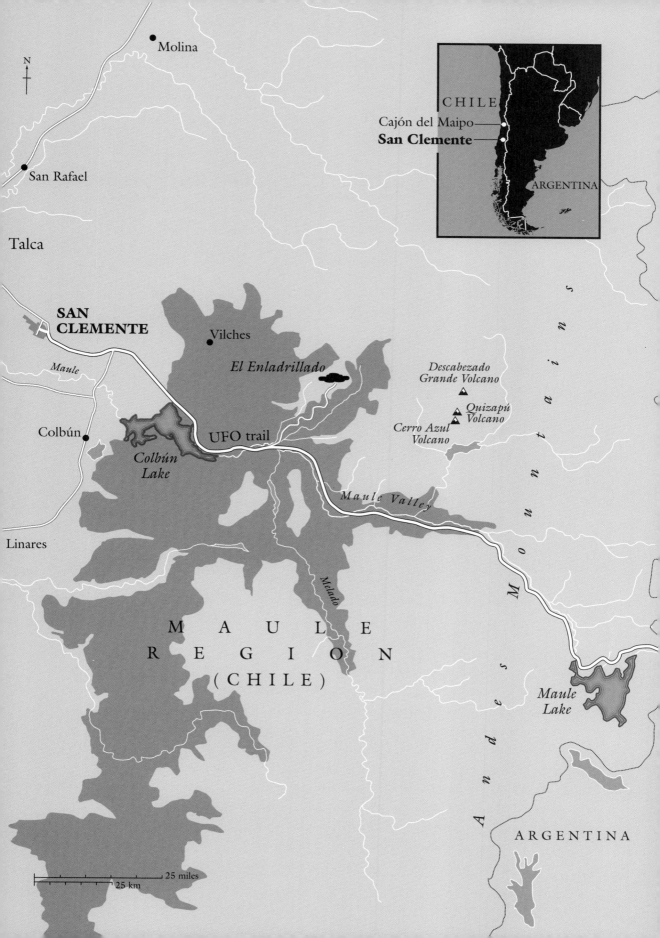

N

Molina

San Rafael

Talca

CHILE

Cajón del Maipo
San Clemente

ARGENTINA

SAN CLEMENTE

Vilches

El Enladrillado

Descabezado
Grande Volcano

Quizapú
Volcano

Cerro Azul
Volcano

Maule

Colbún

UFO trail

Colbún
Lake

Maule Valley

Linares

Melado

M A U L E

R E G I O N

(C H I L E)

Maule
Lake

A
n
d
e
s

M
o
u
n
t
a
i
n
s

ARGENTINA

25 miles

25 km

Giant's Causeway in Ireland – another epic and strange geometric stone flatbed that has an endless trail of lore and mystery. From El Enladrillado, you can see three volcanoes, one of which was still active up until the 1930s; some believe it to be a sort of landing pad for extraterrestrials due to the vast number of sightings reported here over the decades. It's not without controversy, as in order to be a megalith it would have had to be constructed by someone or something, but many geologists believe it to be a natural formation.

As an interesting aside: some researchers throughout history have believed that humankind largely originated from Antarctica, rather than Africa, and that a catastrophic axial pole shift destroyed the inhabited areas there, forcing the population to move to the Americas and the rest of the world. One of these people was Robert Rengifo, a Chilean professor whose work was discussed at the Scientific Society of Chile in the early 1900s. He believed that the inhabited places of the Antarctic region were, in fact, the legendary lost

LEFT: The beautiful Colbun Lake in Maule, Chile.

city of Atlantis. This could explain how a previous civilization in the area was so advanced that it had the ability to create a massive and complex megalith such as El Enladrillado. It's a highly controversial theory to have, but, to be fair, it's not the only ancient site here in Chile that alters how we think about the development and population of the human race. Monte Verde, a wondrous archaeological site in southern Chile, has now proved to show signs that humans inhabited the area up to 14,000 years ago. Rengifo may have been on to something.

The density of observed unexplainable aerial phenomena here led to a formal investigative government body being formed in 1997 – the CEFAA (Comité de Estudios de Fenómenos Aéreos Anómalos – the Committee for the Study of Anomalous Aerial Phenomena). They cover approximately 12 million square miles (32 million sq km), within which they essentially receive reported UFO cases and analyse them using sound scientific approaches to then generate a report. Their main objective is to help dispel myths and keep the airways safe, but the relationship between ufologists and the government has always been a tenuous one. Many believe that governments the world over have known about UFOs for a long time and have kept the information from the general public, but that seems to be changing. At the time of writing, there has been huge uproar in the news as America began to declassify UFO footage, with many former high-ranking Army and Air Force personnel coming forward with stories of strange encounters. Perhaps a benchmark of how chaotic existence is for us all right now is the observance that a major government came forward to confirm UFO phenomena and it was not even the third wildest thing to happen that week.

Chile experienced its own Roswell-like incident in 1998, when many witnesses saw a strange craft crash into Las Mollacas Hill. The Chilean army investigated, and special envoys from NASA had to get involved, who later requested that information on the case be halted. There are more recent striking incidents. In 2018, the crews of no less than six commercial aircraft all simultaneously witnessed the emergence of three triangular light sources in the sky. At the time it was speculated that it could be secret military craft training or lights reflected from ships below, but it seems unlikely that six whole crews who fly that route all the time would all never have encountered this before and that none of them were able to identify what it was. It's not that experienced flight crew are infallible – they certainly can be mistaken – but that many witnesses with that much combined experience, all observing this occurrence simultaneously, certainly makes it one of the stronger contenders for true UFO experiences.

For the working people of San Clemente, some believe it is all a ploy to drive tourism and want nothing to do with any potential visitors from other planets, but many have stories themselves. Several muleteers (these are people who transport goods via pack animals, particularly mules) have had some of the most bizarre experiences. Eladio Gajardo reported seeing a strong light source go up and down in a whirlwind motion in among the mountains, a movement that couldn't have been performed by a helicopter and had no other accompanying lights or noise. It wasn't a brief encounter either; the whirlwind light continued going up and down for about 20 minutes. His brother also had an experience, but this one wasn't lights or spaceships but an actual being. He said he'd seen a small figure that looked like a monkey walking in mid-air over the treetops of the cordillera, just swinging its shoulders from side to side through the air without being attached to anything, as if levitating. Ufologists believed this to be a 'humanoid', by which they mean something that is person-like in shape but is in fact not human.

It isn't the only UFO report here that concerns a being or creature. In Cajón del Maipo, a canyon area where many bodies of water converge to create great lakes and mountain ranges, a mountaineer by the name of Claudio Pastén was visiting a particular lagoon, El Morado. There, he reported seeing two 'huge lights' settle over the basin of water and as soon as he tried to get the attention of the two German tourists with him the lights changed course and dipped into the water, causing the entire lagoon to illuminate. When the light faded a craft suddenly emerged from the water and it left 'two beings of great stature' standing there. This report came in 1997.

Another young man, this time one who works in transport services, named Sebastian Riquelme, had an experience while out driving in Vilches. He was with his girlfriend, who was pregnant at the time, travelling along a road in their pick-up truck. He says that suddenly, out of nowhere, came a red light, hovering several feet above the ground. They slowed down and flashed their truck lights at it; as soon as they did, the light began to expand and get larger. Sebastian says that he felt paralyzed and unable to move and that it went on for a long period of time. He felt so frozen that he never even thought to reach for his phone; all he could do was watch in horror.

Even one of the mayors of this province had encounters as a young boy. Agreed fifteen, Juan Rojas was on a school trip in the 1970s, and during the trip a classmate became injured and needed to be carried back during the night in order to receive medical attention. He said that the group were followed by an oval-shaped object that was lit up at many points, and that this object followed them the whole night, until exhaustion forced them to stop and sleep. Later, in 1990, he would have a second experience when visiting Colbún Lake with his family, where they saw a 'luminous object' emerge from the water.

In 2010, an earthquake measuring 8.8 on the Richter Scale occurred just off the central coast of Chile, at the point where the South American plate is subducted by the Nazca plate, causing tsunamis and killing hundreds of people in its destruction. During this horrendous event, a group of schoolteachers from Talca were camping at the Maule Lagoon when they had an overwhelming, strange experience; they reported that while the ground shook from the after-effects of the earthquake they saw 'vehicles' emerge from the lagoon and fly up into the sky and vanish.

There is a theory among ufologists that San Clemente essentially marks the end of the Inca Road, which connects to Nazca in Peru – another area rich in UFO sightings, historical depictions of UFOs and space-related mythology. The consensus appears to be that many UFO 'hotspot' areas can be linked to one another and that leads to belief that if we are truly experiencing visitors from other planets then they are concentrating on these areas for specific reasons. Chief among them seem to be a focus on large bodies of water that have high mineral quality, areas of large volcanic and tectonic turbulence and ancient stone structures that are monolithic or were created by supreme natural disaster.

The UFO reports from San Clemente don't appear to be slowing down any time soon and it is now hosting annual conferences for enthusiasts to get together and discuss ongoing phenomena and the equipment necessary to capture it. With governments all over the world now starting to declassify information that many feel is challenging what they once wrote off as impossible, the question 'are we alone in the universe?' has become increasingly harder to answer with any sense of absolution.

NEXT: Breathtaking view from Enladrillado.

Wycliffe Well

An area connected to UFO sightings, spies and ancient spiritual worship

In the dusty north western Australian outback stands a diner and petrol service station unlike any other, where travellers may stop for food and to use the last toilet for miles, but it is also where they may find themselves surrounded by hundreds of little extraterrestrial beings. Located about 80 miles (130 km) south of Tennant Creek and 236 miles (380 km) north of Alice Springs, Wycliffe Well is the self-proclaimed UFO capital of Australia. Originally set up as a small watering hole on the route servicing the Overland Telegraph Line in the 1870s, it later became a market garden that serviced a local station, and by the 1930s it was supplying food to local miners. In 1941 it was co-opted as an army farm for soldiers travelling to and from Darwin during the Second World War. The highway began to develop after the war, the place becoming more of a roadhouse. A petrol pump was added in the 1960s and it was then that people began to stop off at Wycliffe Well. Coincidentally, this is about the time that reports came in of strange lights and unearthly sightings in the area.

The region surrounding Wycliffe Well certainly contributes to its mythology. Not far from the roadhouse is Pine Gap – a top-secret intelligence base operated by the CIA and Australian government in order to spy on and collect information from satellites over Russia, China and the Middle East (also the subject of a TV series). It was set up during the Cold War in order to intercept and monitor transmissions concerning nuclear threats but has now evolved to become one of the main war fighting bases for America. With it now employing more than 1,000 staff and housing dozens of satellite dishes in its imposing-looking radomes (giant spherical structures), Pine Gap has participated in and supported every US war since 9/11 and feeds geolocation data to drones used for military strikes. It has come under fire numerous times for controversial data scraping – most notably when former NSA analyst and whistleblower Edward Snowden stated that Pine Gap monitors and intercepts telephone calls, emails, faxes and Internet messages from Australian citizens. But the spies aren't the only secrets here: according to some, Pine Gap is also monitoring communications from extraterrestrial life forms and may be connected to the numerous UFO sightings in the area. It is considered the Australian equivalent of the infamous Area 51 in the States.

While Wycliffe Well had reports of UFO sightings going back more than half a century, it wasn't until the mid-1980s when a man called Lew Farkas bought the buildings and decided

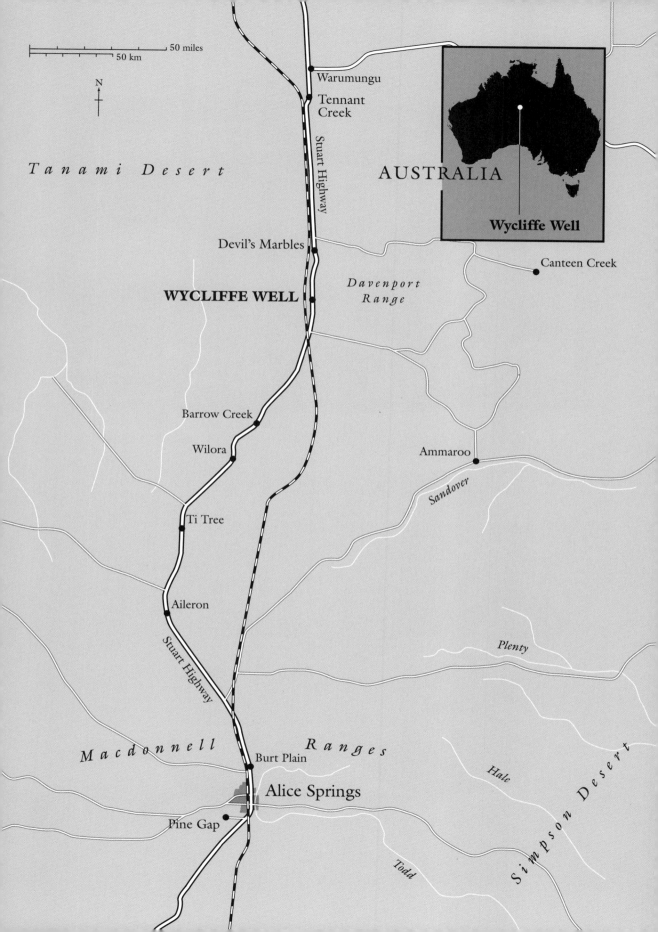

to capitalize on the UFO sightings in the area, that it became the draw it is now. To turn this remote area into a tourist destination, Farkas invested about A\$4 million in the area, adding a railway, a lake, and a 400-seat restaurant. The buildings began to take on a Disney-like appearance, with gigantic, colourful alien murals and hundreds of little grey and green UFOs sticking out of every conceivable surface. It developed into a holiday park with a stage and a beer selection to rival a modern craft brewery.

A guest book was kept here over the years for visitors to write down their own UFO experiences. Farkas himself believed that the UFO phenomena was dense here due to the site being on a convergence of ley lines. That said – if the continuing theory is that UFO phenomena occurs mostly around areas of geological significance, then this area fits the bill. There are two national conservation parks nearby, most notably the Devil's Marbles, or Karlu Karlu, a wildlife area that features peculiar stone monoliths.

Karlu Karlu roughly translates to 'round boulders', and here, gigantic circular stone boulders are stacked precariously on top of other stones, seemingly defying natural creation. But there is a natural explanation for these odd formations. Granite that was formed millions of years ago from the Earth's cooling magma was pushed forth from the ground during shifts in the tectonic plates – the rounding of these blocks was caused by a process known as spheroidal weathering – a chemical exfoliation that only affects the outer few millimetres at a time and is concentrated at the edges.

This area is one of the oldest spiritual sites in the world and is of great significance to Aboriginal Australian people. Karlu Karlu features in many 'dreaming stories', a central one being that the formation was created by *Arrange* (sometimes known as The Devil Man), a mythological being who was travelling through the area while creating a hair-string belt (a traditional piece worn by initiated men) and, as he did so, clumps of hair fell to the ground, which later became the large spheres we see today.

This area is a place of great geological turbulence, ancient stone formations and a density of UFO reports. Ascertaining the connection of the first two is fairly straightforward, as geological turbulence creates striking features that can become intrinsic to the spiritual beliefs of Indigenous people who live on that land – but why this has then become an area with constant phenomena that could be attributed to UFOs (strange lights, flying objects that defy physics, time loss and reports of alien creatures) remains unknown.

LEFT TOP: Wycliffe Well on the Stuart Highway is the UFO Capitol of Australia.

LEFT BOTTOM: Rock formation known as the 'Devil's Marbles' perfectly in balance.

Chapter 6

Cryptids & Creatures

Slaghtaverty Dolmen

The grave of a legendary dwarf-turned vampire

This mythological Irish site is known to some as 'the giant's grave' but it was originally called Abhartach's grave. *Abhartach* is the Irish word for dwarf, a mythological creature that is often interpreted as being human-like or a dark-elf. The dwarf originates from Germanic folklore but it endured after Christianization and descriptions of them vary. Originally depicted as being solely male, but having female family members, later it was portrayed as both male and female. Descriptions in the oldest manuscripts are deliberately vague and that has led some scholars to believe that dwarves were originally disembodied spirits. They are often attributed to mountain areas and are depicted as a skilled race of supernatural beings whose craftsmanship is highly sought. They pop up in Norse mythology quite often; for example, in the story of as the dwarf known as Dvallin forging the cursed legendary sword Tyrfing. In old German lore, several dwarves had the power of invisibility due to a mythological cloak and they played key roles in tales of guarding treasure and giving key items to heroes to help them complete their quests.

The Abhartach of this story was said to be a magician or wizard, a cruel tyrant who plagued the parish of Errigal in Londonderry. He was eventually slain by a neighbouring chieftain (there are some versions that say it was Fionn Mac Cumhail, a hero of Irish folklore, who did so), after which he was buried in a vertical, or standing, posture. The next day he was seen alive and causing more terror than ever. Again, he was killed and buried as before, and again he escaped the grave to engage in more cruelty. The chieftain then consulted a druid who advised that he must be killed a third time and buried headfirst in order to subdue the magical powers that allowed him to rise from the grave. The chief did so and this time the dwarf stayed dead.

This version of the legend was written down in the late 1800s but later versions tell a slightly different tale. In these, the Abhartach rose from the grave to drink the blood of local people and is considered to be more a revenant than a magician or wizard (a revenant is a corpse that has been reanimated from the dead in order to haunt and terrorize the living). The man who killed him consulted a Christian saint rather than a druid and was known as Cathán (this is a surname now anglicized as O'Kane/Kane/Keane). The saint he consulted was one of the *neamh-mhairbh*, the undead vampiric creatures from Celtic mythology,

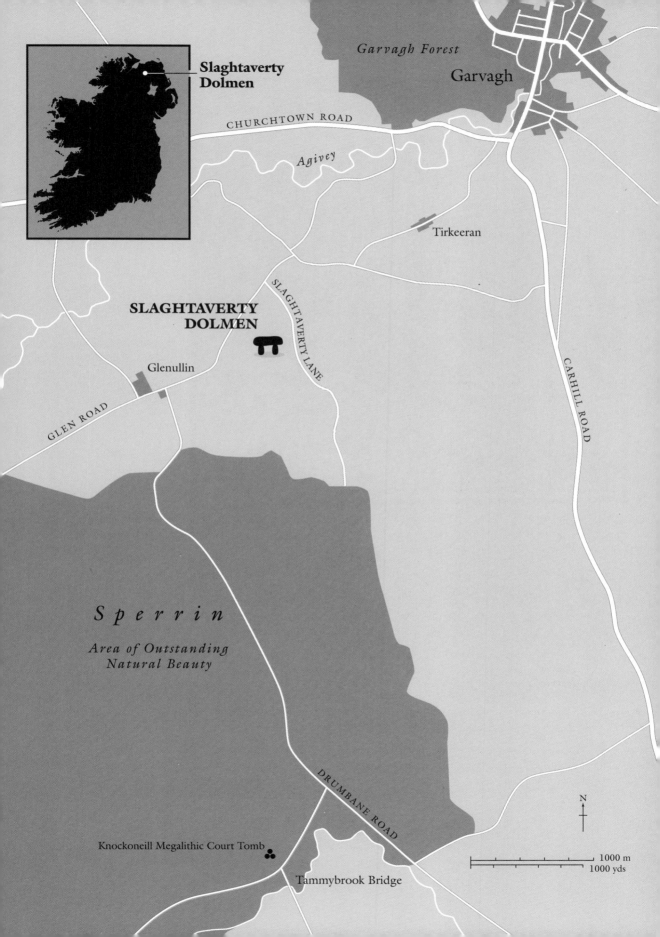

Slaghtaverty Dolmen

Garvagh Forest

Garvagh

CHURCHTOWN ROAD

Agivey

Tirkeeran

SLAGHTAVERTY LANE

SLAGHTAVERTY DOLMEN

Glenullin

GLEN ROAD

CARHILL ROAD

Sperrin

Area of Outstanding Natural Beauty

DRUMBANE ROAD

N

Knockoneill Megalithic Court Tomb

Tammybrook Bridge

1000 m
1000 yds

who told him the only way to kill him was with a sword made of yew tree and burying him upside down. His grave then had to be surrounded with thorns, with a giant stone placed on top.

The grave site today is still composed of a large rock and two smaller rocks beneath a hawthorn bush. Reportedly, in 1997, the land was set to be cleared but the workers had their chainsaw fail three times while trying to cut down the hawthorn that arches over the grave. When they tried to move the large rock that makes up the dolmen, the steel chain snapped and cut the hand off of one of the men, leaving blood to pour into the ground. There have been many arguments about whether or not this legend influenced Bram Stoker in his writing of *Dracula* – undeniably the most recognized and definitive vampire tale in modern times. Bram Stoker was Irish, hailing from Dublin, so it is very much possible that he was familiar with the ancient tale of Abhartach and may have used this as an inspiration for *Dracula*. The popular school of thought, though, has always been that *Dracula* was inspired by Vlad III 'The Impaler', a ruler of Wallachia in Romania during the 1400s; his father was Vlad Dracul, 'Vlad the Dragon' in medieval Romanian. Dracula was a given

nickname of Vlad the Impaler and his brutal acts proceeded him as he was said to favour killing his enemies by impaling then on large spikes en masse. However, the accounts of Vlad's brutality should be examined with caution as many were anecdotal; we see the first true emphasis of torture and psychopathy emerge after his death, when accounts of his raids against the Transylvanian Saxons were written retroactively. Bram Stoker was the first to connect ancient Transylvanian superstitions about vampires to the name Dracula but the texts he used were limited in their information and so he would have known very little about Vlad the Impaler. His actual notes for the book show that he chose the name Dracula simply from pieces of random information about the history of Wallachia and his Romanian origin because of the horrendous war campaigns by Atilla the Hun. There is no mention at all of Vlad the Impaler.

If we examine the lore of what it means to be a *neamh-mhairbh* in Irish mythology, we may get a better understanding of how this could intersect with vampirism lore as a whole. The word *neamh* is Irish for 'heaven', which is why you often see it used as a name (particularly for girls), and the word *mhairbh* is the Irish word for 'dead'. However, when *neamh* is written as *neamh-* it transforms to mean *un-*, giving us the phrase *un-dead*. These creatures come to be from someone using magic to reanimate a corpse and the earlier lore does not paint them as vampires, nor do they have any core vampiric traits, other than being undead. It might actually be more accurate to imagine them as what we would now call a 'zombie'. The tales of these revenants surviving on blood was added later, so if the Abhartach lore was an influence on Stoker's *Dracula* it would have only been on the undead and tyranny components, meaning the blood drinking was drawn from European lore.

Stoker wasn't the only Irish writer to contribute to the vampire legends as we know them now. In 1872 the Irish Gothic writer Sheridan Le Fanu penned the work *Carmilla*. This piece first appeared as a series of stories in literary magazine *The Dark Blue* before being collected together and published as a novella. It predates Stoker's *Dracula* by twenty-six years and features a young woman being preyed upon by a female vampire revealed to be Countess Karnstein. It was not only one of the earliest works of vampire fiction but is a fine example of Sapphic literature.

Vampire lore trickled into popular Western culture from Eastern European mythology shortly after the Renaissance period and its popularity is in part due to the invention of the printing press. Earlier in this book the legend and death of Countess Elizabeth Báthory came up, who was said to have bathed in blood. That took place in the early 1600s but the morbid details of her story didn't truly materialize until the mid-1700s, and it was shortly after this time that some of the key vampire tales started to emerge from the same area. As the Habsburg Empire expanded, stories of blood-drinking, undead monsters started to roll out of what we would now call Transylvania, Romania, Hungary and Serbia. The Balkans as a whole contributed perhaps the most to contemporary vampire mythology, although similar creatures appear in many other mythologies over the globe.

In 1725, a peasant man known as Peter Blagojevic died in the town of Kisilova (believed to be Kisiljevo) in the part of Serbia that had previously been ruled by the Ottoman Empire but had temporarily come under Habsburg jurisdiction. Shortly afterwards, many other people in the village fell ill and died within 24 hours of their first reported symptoms. In just over a week nine people had died and witnesses stated that the dead had reported seeing Blagojevic in their rooms the night before their deaths. His wife also had reported him coming to visit her to ask for his shoes. In a different version, Blagojevic came back to his house and demanded his son give him food and drink; when the son refused, he attacked and murdered him. The village went into a craze and exhumed the coffin of Blagojevic to look for signs that he was in fact still living and feeding on the villagers. They reported to officials that if they did not act quickly then the whole village would be wiped out and that this had actually happened previously when the town was still under the Ottoman Empire. When his body was examined, it was reported to have new nails, new skin and his beard had grown longer, and there was blood in his mouth. This was concurrent with local beliefs about vampires and so he was staked through the heart, which caused 'fresh blood to pour forth' from his ears and mouth. The body was then burnt.

This event was reported by a Viennese newspaper known today as *Die Wiener Zeitung* alongside a similar Serbian case that had occurred in 1726 in Trstenik when Arnold Paole was believed to have come back as a vampire and killed sixteen people in his village. Both cases sparked a massive interest in vampires throughout the Victorian era in England, Germany and France – likely due to the credibility lent to them because Austrian authorities had been involved in both cases and there were official testimonies given by physicians, which seemed to confirm the existence of such supernatural creatures. What was seen on the corpses (hair growth, blood in the mouth, etc.) is part of what we now know to be the natural process of decomposition.

Apotropaics (items that are used to deflect harm and ward against evil creatures) come up often in vampiric lore. The most popular two found in European beliefs would be garlic and, later, the sign of the Christian cross. In some parts of Eastern Europe mustard seeds were sprinkled on the tops of dwellings to ward off potential vampires. Certain types of plants could be grown over graves, or branches could be placed in homes to cause harm to vampires, most notably the wild rose or hawthorn. This may explain the hawthorn found at Abhartach's grave; it was either already growing there and this influenced the legend taking on the vampire qualities, or the instructions to surround the grave with thorns to stop reanimation resulted in the planting of it. Hawthorn comes up a remarkable amount in vampire cases all over Europe, although in this Irish case, yew was the chosen wood for the stake. The term 'vampire' didn't appear until the 1700s and is believed to be influenced by the French term *vampyre*, which is in turn influenced by the Slavic use of *vampir* and *upyr*. Trying to categorize a being as a vampire in the last few hundred years has seemed to hinge on two core aspects – they must rise from the dead and they must drink blood. If they rise or reanimate without the blood drinking then this is a revenant, which is found in the mythology of nearly every civilization on Earth. There are also stories of blood-drinking evil creatures in hundreds of cultures, but they were often closer to demons or shape-shifters. The older stories are almost all clearly depictions of revenants, but they have been retroactively categorized as vampires from the 1700s onwards. We see this in Celtic mythology, with tales of evil fae creatures now classed as vampires. This may be the case with the legend of Abhartach too, as it begins as a tale of a dwarf or wizard and then becomes that of a revenant and later a vampire. This is also supported by the lack of general vampire mythology in Irish history. But please don't remove the stones to find out!

PREVIOUS LEFT: Vlad the Impaler, dining in the midst of impaled bodies.
PREVIOUS RIGHT: The grave stones beneath the hawthorn tree.
NEXT: This rumoured vampire grave remains in a field in County Derry.

Al Madam
Ghost Town

Abandoned desert town haunted by a jinn

In the desert emirate of Sharjah, roughly an hour's drive away from the glistening skyscrapers and flash super-cars of Dubai, lies the town of Al Madam, a place where the only remarkable feature seems to be its annual shopping festival. However, there is an older part of this town known locally as 'Old Al Madam' or the 'Al Madam Ghost Town' or 'Buried Town'. This little village was constructed in the 1970s to house the Bedouin population, mostly from the tribe of Al Ketbi, but by the 1990s it was abandoned and is now being reclaimed by the sand. Few roofs, walls and trees can be seen in aerial photos, the skeleton of this town the only remaining clue that anyone once lived here at all. But how exactly did it come to be abandoned? It's a topic of much speculation.

The village has two rows of houses and a mosque, many still with rusty iron gates and open, glassless window spaces where interested travellers can climb through – though they should be mindful of the wandering scorpions who live here. Inside there are colourful tiles and abandoned furniture, peeling paint and decaying murals, and sand piled up to the ceiling as the desert slowly reclaims this ghost town. The obvious answer to why everyone fled would be the harsh living conditions, from the encroaching desert to the lack of reliable electricity, exacerbated by a lack of infrastructure. You can imagine as cities like Dubai exploded into the sprawling luxury they are now, people left these tiny desert towns in search of a better life.

But there is another theory – that they were driven away by the creatures known as the *jinn*.

The *jinn* (romanized as djinn) are supernatural beings found in Islamic beliefs that are essentially a type of demi-god. They exist on a plane of reality that humans are not partial to and they possess a variety of powers, notably shape-shifting. They are not immortal gods, however, since they can be killed in combat by a human. The *jinn* appeared first in pre-Islamic Arabian mythology and were possibly a demonization of older Pagan beliefs, which would also explain the potential Aramaic origins of the word. They are mentioned twenty-nine times in the Qur'an but are demoted from deities to minor spirits, likely to discourage further worship. Some texts state that the *jinn* were a race that inhabited Earth before humans. People in pre-Islamic Arabia were said to summon them to devolve knowledge,

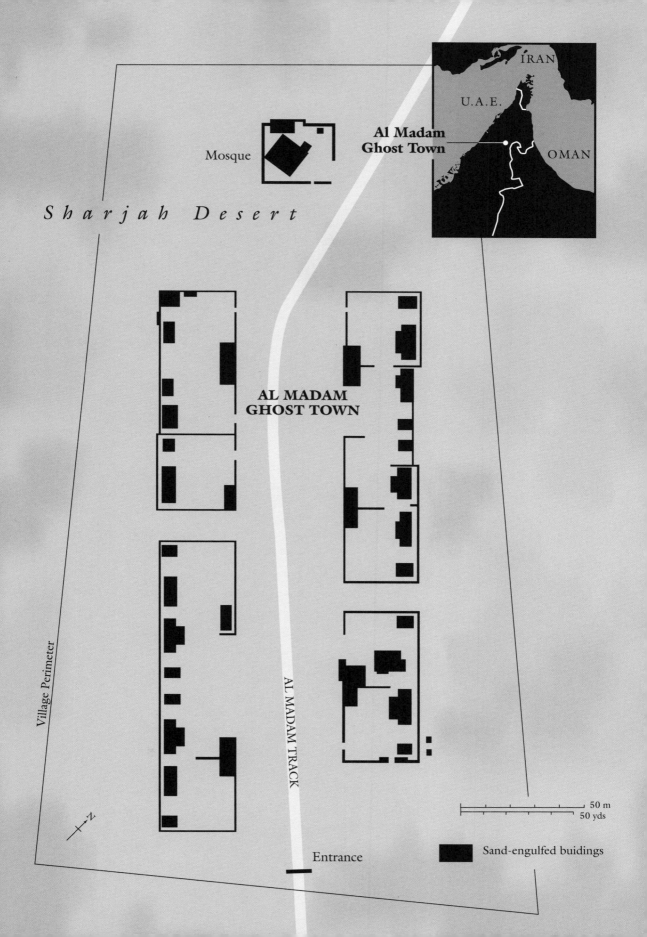

IRAN

U.A.E.

**Al Madam
Ghost Town**

OMAN

Mosque

S h a r j a h   D e s e r t

**AL MADAM
GHOST TOWN**

Village Perimeter

AL MADAM TRACK

N

50 m
50 yds

Entrance

Sand-engulfed buidings

offer protection, or enact deeds on their behalf. Western people know these creatures as wish-granting genies. They are said to be composed of thin and barely corporeal bodies that can take on any shape or form at will. They are often depicted in the form of a snake or as a human with hooves for feet, but they have also taken on the appearance of lizards and scorpions.

The abandoned old Al Madam ghost town has reports of one *jinn* in particular haunting it – Umm al-Duwais. This particular supernatural entity draws on a primary tenet of folklore: the siren. We all know these types of tales – that a beautiful but strange woman is actually a powerful creature or evil entity in disguise, whose job it is to lure men into the darkness and dispatch them to hell or feed on them to gain more power. The Umm al-Duwais embodies this trope in Emirati culture. It's worth noting that not all *jinn* are evil; they tend to be a more neutral force that displays free will and are subject to being judged by Allah, just as humans are. Umm al-Duwais takes on the form of a beautiful woman with long, dark hair, but it's said that her sweet, intoxicating scent is what really lures people in. She is said to appear as a lost young woman looking for help; she roams the streets at night where she can prey on men looking to commit acts of lust. Once a man is lured into her body, she changes form to that of a warped old woman and slices off his head.

She was likely constructed to scare men into being faithful to their wives and put fear into those who would go out looking for sexual intimacy with strangers. There is a saying in Emirati culture that reflects this:

الليل مب حق البشر

'*The night is not for humans.*' One story states that a man who encountered her lived because he began to chant the name of Allah out of fear. At hearing this holy name, the creature cowered and ran away. Of course, this fits with most stories of defeating evil creatures; in the same way that vampires are scared of Christian crosses and those possessed by demons can be exorcised by reciting passages from the Bible, this *jinn* can be scared away by chanting the name of Allah. There is a belief among some that *jinn* can actually possess a human person and it seems to be an enduring belief as in 2016 there were cases of widespread 'mania' among Pakistani women, that were attributed to them being possessed by a *jinn*. But then, throughout history, women have been accused of being corrupted by some kind of evil whenever they display even the most minor characteristic that violates the parameters assigned to them by men. If you look at historic medical cases, many women suffering from mental health issues, diseases that affected hormone levels or reproductive organ-related health problems (such as PCOS) were simply labelled 'hysterical' and were locked away to die, so they didn't inconvenience anyone. It's imperative to contextualize paranormal beliefs within the cultural settings and sociological parameters in order to understand how they come to be.

LEFT: A historical building in the derelict Al Madam ghost town.
ABOVE: The buildings are being slowly swallowed by the desert.

The Qiu Mansion

Abandoned mansion with nightmare animals

At the start of the twentieth century two migrant brothers, Qiu Xingshan and Qiu Weiqing, were living as peasants while working under a German employer in the dye industry in China. When the First World War broke out, in 1914, their employer fled, leaving the two brothers behind. With no draft system in place, they were free from being drawn into the war. The price and value of dye skyrocketed and the Qiu brothers came into a proverbial gold mine. They would go on to become millionaires in their city and live lives of great opulence that would rival that of kings and legendary gangsters, but it all ended in tragedy; decades later, this horror would become supernatural fear.

The brothers built a mansion complex in 1920 that consisted of two palaces, the East Block and the West Block, one for each brother to live with their family and friends. The estate was surrounded by magnificent gardens that housed many exotic animals – Burmese tigers, crocodiles on the banks of the lake and peacocks among the magnolia trees. It is these animals and birds that would play a central role in the ghost stories many years later.

At the height of their notoriety and success the brothers suddenly vanished and were never heard from again. The mansions fell into disrepair and the once-decadent gardens became overgrown and wild with barren branches. The animals were either sold off or eaten as the local area fell into the grip of a dire famine. During the Second World War, the site was used to house students from Minli Middle school, and later, the West Block was razed with only the East Block remaining. In 2002, an international conglomerate company, HKRI, acquired the site and began developing it into a commercial complex, but the East Block was still being used as a school and they eventually had to move the entire building less than a mile (570 m) to the south of the site, where it remains now, renamed as Cha House.

It was during this construction period that the ghostly tales and bizarre incidents erupted. In the summer of 2009, workers from the site were turning up at the local hospital with what can only be described as bite wounds. These wounds were verified by a nurse, Li Fei, who oversaw the cases coming in at night to Yueyang Hospital. A thorough search of the premises was conducted and no wild animals were found, but the workers remained too frightened to return. The night terrors evolved when employees at a nearby Four Seasons hotel began reporting that they were seeing nightmarish animals manifesting out of thin

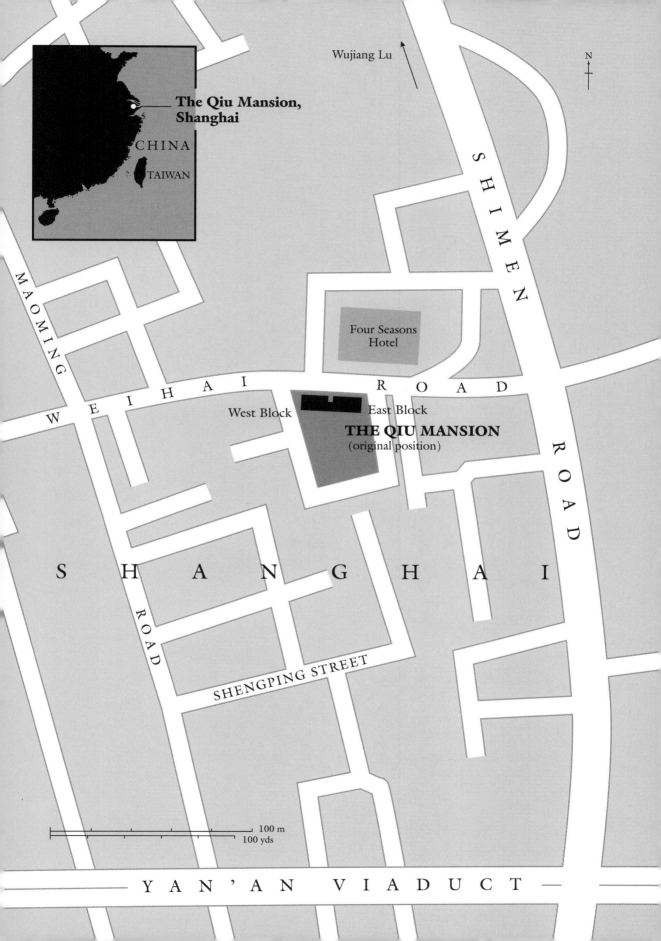

The Qiu Mansion,
Shanghai

CHINA

TAIWAN

Wujiang Lu

N

SHIMEN

ROAD

Four Seasons
Hotel

MAOMING

WEIHAI   ROAD

West Block   East Block

THE QIU MANSION
(original position)

S   H   A   N   G   H   A   I

ROAD

SHENGPING STREET

100 m
100 yds

Y A N ' A N   V I A D U C T

RIGHT: Exterior of The Qiu Mansion in Shanghai, China. Built by two brothers who were peasants-turned-millionaires.

air while they worked the nightshift – these animals would appear across the street in the derelict building site, roam around the grounds and then vanish. They weren't the only ones to see fantastical beasts at the site. One Mrs Ye, who lived down an alley just off Wujiang Lu, right next to the construction site, reported that she saw a monstrous 'dragon' climbing along the arm of one of the cranes at the site. Things took a bloodier turn that August, when a mason working at the site snapped with no prior warning and went at his manager with a hammer. When asked what had caused this sudden violent outburst, he simply replied that 'the lizards' had made him do it.

Then, the cases seemed to suddenly stop and renovations were completed without further complication. It's difficult to find scientific explanations for what happened. Urban myth and local lore could make people frightened enough to imagine they were seeing creatures in the dark when nothing was really there, but physical bite marks? It's not often that ghosts bite. That's much harder to rationalize away. We have to trust that there was a thorough inspection of the site for animals, but without photographs of the bites an assessment of what might have caused them cannot be carried out.

| Otago, New Zealand | 45.0802° S, 168.5740° E |

Lake Wakatipu

A lake that holds the heart of a giant Māori taniwha

This 112 square-mile (290 sq km) inland lake is the third largest in New Zealand and has a remarkable depth of 1,377 feet (420 m) at its deepest point. It sits in the south west point of Otago and is overlooked by two mountain ranges, the Remarkables and the Hectors. This site of natural beauty actually doubled for Loch Ness in the 2007 cryptid fantasy film *The Water Horse* and many will recognize it as Amon Hen from the *Lord of the Rings* films. The original Māori name for the lake is *Whakatipu-wai-Māori*. It's believed to come from the Waitaha people but it is so ancient that the direct translation has been lost. It has been interpreted in the past as 'bay of spirits', 'growing bay' and 'sacred vessel'. But there is another translation of the name that links it to the supernatural.

Waka would be a contraction meaning 'trough' and *tipua* is a shape-shifting creature from Māori mythology that is classically associated with natural landmarks, particularly mountains and trees. The word *tipua* can simply mean strange, uncanny and supernatural but can also denote a demon, evil or feared object and you'll see it used in conjunction with the names of some of the most prominent beings in Māori mythology. A core example of this would be *Whiro-te-tipua*, the ruler of the underworld and embodiment of all darkness and evil (what would usually be interpreted as the devil in Western belief systems). When people die it is *Whiro* who eats their bodies when they arrive in the underworld and this causes him to gain strength; that is why Māori beliefs recommend people be cremated rather than buried, so that their corpses cannot feed *Whiro*.

The *tipua* used in the naming of this lake is a reference to a giant mythological being whose death is supposed to have caused the lake to form. The being is known as a *taniwha* – a massive supernatural creature that often resides in dark caves and deep waters. Some are great protectors of sacred lands and some are evil creatures that kidnapped women to take as wives. People would leave offerings to appease them, often the first sweet potato or taro of the harvest. Belief in the *taniwha* has played an important role in Māori culture even in modern times. In 2002 the people of the Ngāti Naho tribe successfully challenged the route planning of State Highway 1 in order to have it diverted away from the sacred grounds where they believe the *taniwha* that protects them lives.

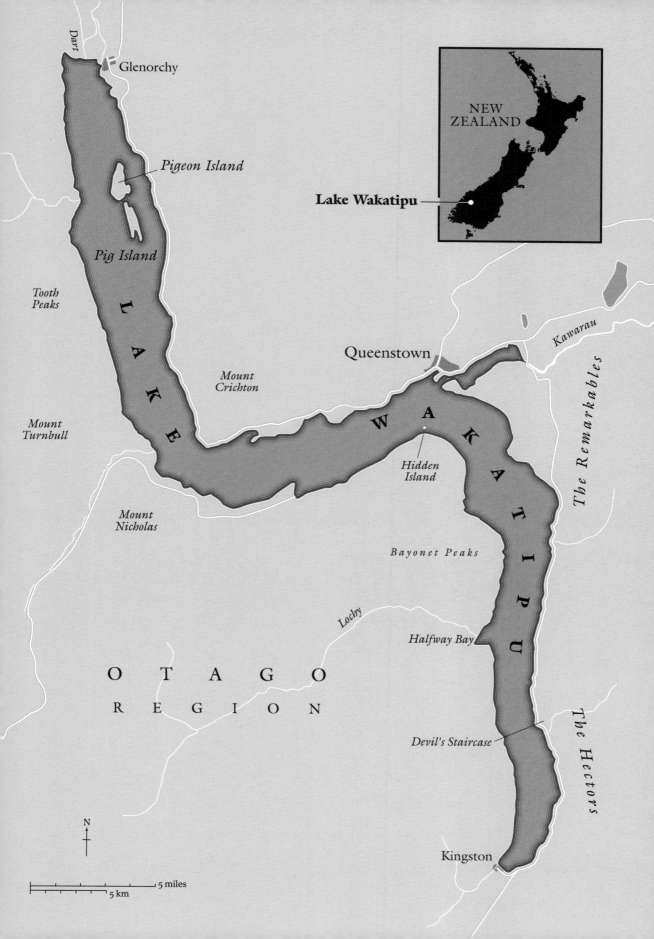

Dart

Glenorchy

Pigeon Island

Pig Island

*Tooth
Peaks*

L A K E

*Mount
Crichton*

*Mount
Turnbull*

*Mount
Nicholas*

NEW
ZEALAND

Lake Wakatipu

Queenstown

Kawarau

W A K A T I P U

*Hidden
Island*

The Remarkables

Bayonet Peaks

Lochy

Halfway Bay

O T A G O

R E G I O N

Devil's Staircase

The Hectors

N

Kingston

5 miles

5 km

The story of this lake's *taniwha* claims that long ago there were two lovers, Manata and Matakauri, who lived in a village here. Unfortunately, their love had to be kept secret as it was forbidden for Manata, the daughter of a great tribal chief, to be with Matakauri, who was only a commoner. One night a *taniwha* called Matau came down from the mountains and hills as all slept and ventured into the village. He stole Manata, tying her to him with an enchanted cord and carried her back up to his dark caves. Manata's father was enraged and summoned every eligible man in the village to rescue his daughter, promising that whoever brought Manata back safely would be awarded her hand in marriage. Many were too afraid to go after the giant *taniwha* but Matakauri was deeply in love with Manata and so he ventured out on the heels of the north west wind to search the mountains for his stolen love.

When he finally found the giant's cave, he discovered Matau fast asleep with Manata still tied to him. He tried to cut the cord but it was preserved with powerful magic. Manata begged him to leave, fearing that if the *taniwha* woke up it would kill them both. As Manata began to cry the love in her tears dissolved the magic cord and they were able to escape. Once safely back in the village the people feared that the giant would return to cause more trouble so after Manata and Matakauri were wed, the young man ventured back into the mountains. There he found the giant lulled to sleep by the warm winds; he set a gigantic

fire and as the winds fanned the flames it became an all-consuming inferno. The *taniwha*'s body burnt for so long at such an intense heat that it left behind a great crater. This filled with the rains and so Lake Wakatipu was formed. It is said that Glenorchy rests at his head, Queenstown at his knees, Kingston at his feet and that his heart still remains beating beneath Pigeon Island. It is this ever-beating heart of the giant that causes the seiche (the constant rising and lowering of the lake's water levels).

Another version of this legend says that Matau is not dead, but rather asleep at the bottom of the lake, or in the sediment beneath it. A non-mythological explanation for the lake's seiche is the S or lightning-bolt shape, which causes, rather than a tide, a standing wave to form. This means that the water levels rise and fall approximately 10 cm every 25 minutes. It's important to note that some would categorize Matau as a lake monster, similar to the Loch Ness Monster in Scotland, but this is categorically incorrect. Nessie is a cryptid, and by that I mean a cryptozoological creature that has sightings independent of a belief system. Matau is a *taniwha*, one of many, which serve a purpose not just in the lore but in the actual everyday belief systems of the Māori people.

ABOVE: Lake Wakatipu, Queenstown, Otago, New Zealand.

The Mines of Donbas

Mines that have their own supernatural tyrant or protector

'Donbas' is a portmanteau of Donets Coal Basin and is a large industrial area in eastern Ukraine bordering with Russia. The region is predominantly known for the heavy industries of coal mining and metallurgy and has been a highly conflicted and important economic area since the nineteenth century. The region can trace its lineage back to the first Indo-European people and was once populated by many nomadic tribes, though it did not have its first official town settled until 1676. Parts of the area have passed constantly between Ukrainian jurisdiction and Russian occupation, and it was also occupied and subsequently decimated by the Nazis for several years during the Second World War. These ancient mines are home to a very particular type of mythology that centres around a spirit known as a *Shubin*.

There's no definitive etymology of the word *Shubin* but it is believed to possibly be the name of a former miner who died and now walks the mines as a ghost, often seen in a fur coat and carrying a torch, where he protects the other miners by burning off the excess gas that builds up in pockets (these gas pockets are known as firedamp). It could also be the name of a cruel master of the mines, who murdered several men down there in the dark. Some mining towns hold the view that the *Shubin* is a positive force who protects the people who work there and must be honoured; others view it as a wicked spirit.

The stories of the 'good *Shubin*' often paint this entity as a former mining master who had a great gift for predicting when a tunnel collapse was about to happen. He would go down into the mine first, ahead of his men, and if he felt something was not quite right he would warn them. This act of warning the miners carried over into the afterlife it would seem, as miners refer to the *Shubin* when they feel they are in danger. One miner reported the lights going out suddenly due to power problems and in the complete darkness he became disorientated and could not find his way to the exit. He saw the blinking light of a man holding a torch and, even though he was afraid, he followed the light and was led to safety. He believed this light to be the torch of the *Shubin*.

The 'bad *Shubin*' mythos seems to populate the mines in the city of Luhansk and in the Ural Mountain region of Russia. In Luhansk, they say that a man came to the town looking for work and came across several drunken miners in a bar, who said they would hire him to work the mines if he was able to go down with a torch by himself and walk a few feet in

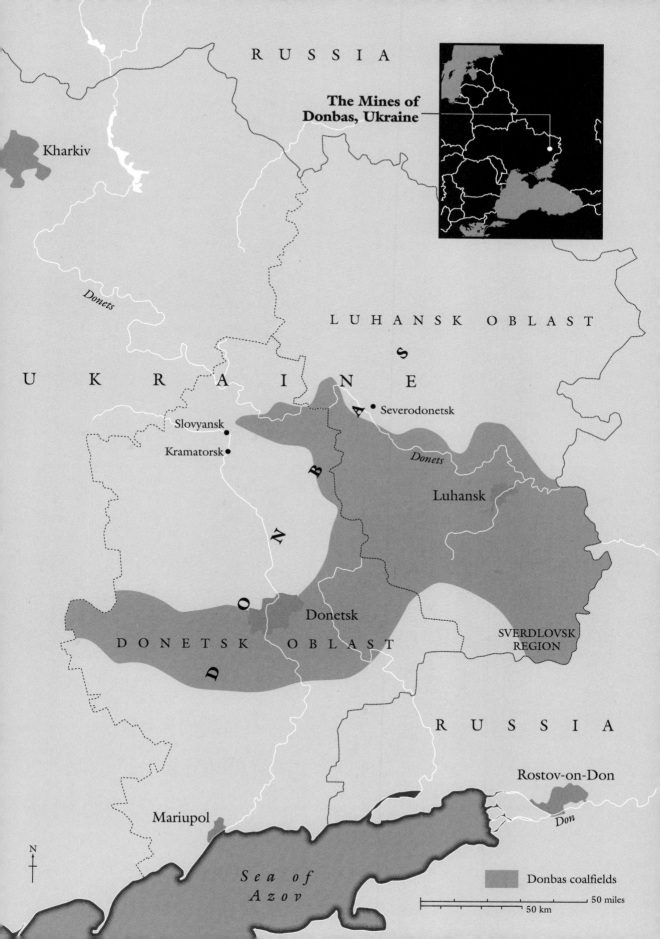

RUSSIA

**The Mines of
Donbas, Ukraine**

Kharkiv

Donets

LUHANSK OBLAST

U K R A I N E

Slovyansk

Kramatorsk

Severodonetsk

Donets

Luhansk

D O N B A S

DONETSK OBLAST

Donetsk

SVERDLOVSK
REGION

RUSSIA

Rostov-on-Don

Don

Mariupol

N

*Sea of
Azov*

Donbas coalfields

50 miles

50 km

ATLAS OF PARANORMAL PLACES

the dark without being afraid. The true nature of their offer was not to test his resolve, but to use him as a fatal way of testing whether or not methane gas had built up in the mines overnight. They figured it would be better that a stranger die than one of their own when they returned to work in the morning. When gas builds up in pockets it may just burn, rather than explode, and so to deal with this they gave the stranger a fur coat as protection. Unfortunately, the gas build-up was extreme and a fatal explosion did occur, killing the man and resulting in his ghost haunting the mines, constantly seeking revenge for what the miners did to him. The belief in this evil *Shubin* was so strong that in 2002 the head of the Orthodox Church in Luhansk, His Eminence Metropolitan Кобзев, descended into the mines in order to say prayers and bless the place so that this evil spirit would be driven out.

In some Ukrainian mines, the *Shubin* is believed to appear as a beautiful woman. She is often referred to as the *Bira Koroleva* (the White Queen). There's a legend in the Sverdlovsk region that a miner went missing and was finally found in one of the mine shafts – naked and delirious. He said that he had encountered the *Bira Koroleva* and that she had tried to trick him, but her great beauty eventually drove him to lose all sense of rationality and he went insane. Several more miners from that area then also proceeded to lose their minds and were all taken to a mental hospital, all raving about the 'White Queen'. People would pass this mental hospital and mock the afflicted men, calling them the 'White Kings' of the mines. Since then, there have been no further reports of this female embodiment of the *Shubin*.

The *Bira Koroleva* is not the only siren-type creature in Ukrainian mythology. In fact there is a creature in Slavic Paganism that takes the form of a pretty young girl with long hair who lives in the mountain caves by rivers and forests, where she plants flowers and lures men away and then tickles them to death. The fact that these creatures tickle their prey to death is bizarre enough but their appearance is also interesting: they do not cast a shadow or have a reflection in running water, traits usually only found in vampire lore. These creatures are known as the *Mavka*, but the sub-species of them known as the *Nyavka* have no back. Meaning from the front they appear as pretty young girls, but when they turn around you can see their entire spine and organs exposed. The *Mavkas* and *Nyavkas* are different to the *Bira Koroleva* as their evil is not intentional; when they see a young man they go into a kind of trance and do not come to their senses until it is too late and they have already killed them.

The *Mavka* are found primarily in central Ukraine while the *Nyavka* are native to western Ukraine, where the mountains and rivers are considered more dangerous. This connection to the land puts them somewhere between the classification of a nymph, a succubus and a siren. The *Shubin*, in both its male and female form, would be classified as a ghost but arguably it is more the embodying spirit of an entire place (the mines, specifically the Donbas mining region) which then takes on a different form, depending on its intentions.

LEFT TOP: The mines of Donbas have an estimated reserve of 60 billion tonnes of coal.
LEFT BOTTOM: Iron sculpture of a mine ghost in the park of forged figures.

Gangkhar Puensum

The land of the thunder dragon and many mythological beasts

The kingdom of Bhutan is a sovereign, land-locked state in South Asia, located between India and China. Its origins are shrouded in mythology and mystery and it is estimated that it may have been a country as early as 2000 BCE. However, very little was written down prior to the arrival of Buddhism from Tibet in the seventh century and most of what did survive was destroyed in a fire in the 1800s. Bhutan is a mountainous country that is often referred to as '*Druk Yul*', the land of the thunder dragon, and it is home to one very particular mountain, widely regarded to be the highest unclimbed mountain in the world – Gangkhar Puensum. Written in the native Dzongkha as གངས་དཀར་སྤུན་གསུམ, it translates to 'white peak of the three spiritual brothers'. It remains unclimbed, not just because of its treacherous face and biting winds, but because it is actually forbidden to do so. To understand why this legendary mountain is forbidden from humans conquering it, we need to look at the spiritual culture and deep sacred mythology of Bhutan as a whole.

Gangkhar Puensum has an elevation of 24,840 feet (7,571 m), ranking it the fortieth highest mountain in the world, but it has only ever seen five attempted expeditions. Starting in the 1980s all attempts failed for various reasons, including not being able to find the mountain at all due to incomplete maps and extreme weather phenomena. In 1999, a Japanese-led expedition team approaching from the Chinese border side was able to successfully summit the second highest peak, Liankang Kangri. They were almost thwarted as their permit to explore was revoked by the Bhutan government. This was in addition to Bhutan's outright ban of the exploration and climbing of mountains higher than 20,000 feet (6,096 m) in 1994, followed by all and any mountaineering being banned absolutely by the government in 2003. This might seem extreme and one might assume that it was related to safety reasons, but you would be wrong: it is actually a result of spiritual and supernatural beliefs.

Bhutan's governance has always been directly influenced by supernatural belief, going all the way back to 810 CE when the Buddhist saint Padmasambhava came to Bhutan from India, and after 'subduing eight classes of demons', was able to convert the king to Buddhism. More than 75 per cent of the population here is Buddhist, and being a sparsely populated country that practised isolation (they only began to admit outsiders in small

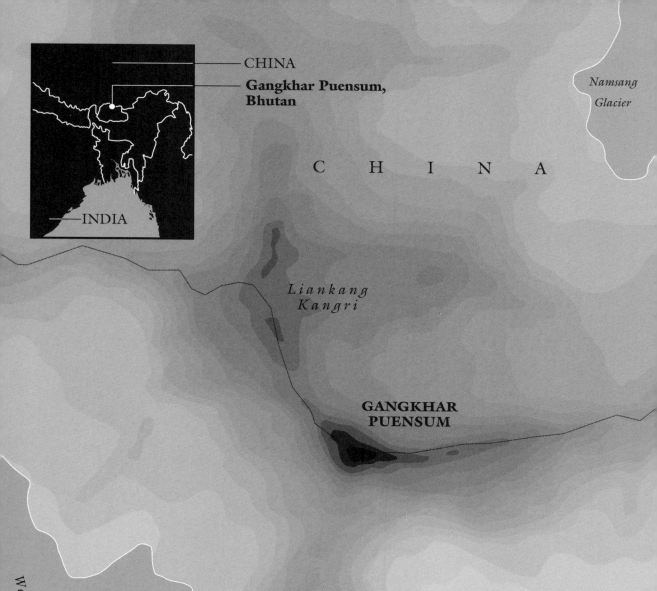

CHINA

Gangkhar Puensum,
Bhutan

INDIA

C H I N A

*Namsang
Glacier*

*Liankang
Kangri*

**GANGKHAR
PUENSUM**

West Gangkhar Puensum Glacier

Gangkhar Puensum Glacier

B H U T A N

2500 m
2500 yds

N

groups in the late decades of the twentieth century), it has been able to preserve its ancient customs and culture. Here you will find brightly coloured Buddhist prayer flags fluttering up and down the mountainside but if you look closely you will also find a small white flag at the top of each home. This is to signify that this person has given an offering to the deity or god that governs that area.

Bhutan has a unique wildlife sanctuary, as it is the only country in the world to have a preserve specially for a mythological creature – the Yeti. This giant, legendary creature is sometimes known as 'the abominable snowman' by Westerners but in Bhutan it is called the 'migoi'. It is known not only for its giant size and strength but also for its magical ability to turn invisible or travel backwards in order to stop it from being tracked by humans. The *migoi* are described as exuding a foul odour and being reddish-brown or grey in colour. In the Sakteng region of eastern Bhutan, you can find the wildlife sanctuary set up to preserve the *migoi*'s land, where they are free to roam among the pine and rhododendron. The Himalayan mountains as a whole are considered to be the sacred land of the yeti or *migoi* and this includes the forbidden Gangkhar Puensum peak.

The creature that lies at the centre of Bhutanese culture, however, is the dragon. In Buddhism, dragons represent power and the sound they make as they thunder through the sky is said to awaken all from delusions and increase the knowledge and wisdom you can gain from listening. They are creatures that represent awareness of that which we cannot see. The thunder dragon can be seen on the flag of Bhutan against the yellow and orange background, flying as it clutches a large jewel in its claws. This jewel symbolizes the wealth and prosperity of the country of Bhutan, the dragon itself personifying the mythology and sacred spirituality. The thunder dragon is sung about in the national anthem of Bhutan 'Druk Tsendhen' and the leaders and kings are addressed as Druk Gyalpo, 'the Thunder Dragon Kings'. Legend has it that Bhutan got its native name Druk Yul when a meditation master travelled to the land in order to set up a spiritual centre – while there, he witnessed nine dragons perched on the mountains. They flew off as he approached, creating a deafening thunder clap as they flew through the sky.

The sacred mountains here are believed to be inhabited not only by legendary creatures but also revered deities and gods, and it is the desire of the people of Bhutan to preserve these places and not allow humans to trample through the peaks of the gods, lest they bring calamity and retribution down upon the country. Looking at the level of pollution and damage left on nearby Mount Everest by tourists and mountaineers, it seems a perfectly sensible decision.

In the traditional Bhutanese pantheon of deities, there is one seen as the chief protecting god of the country, Palden Lhamo. This goddess is usually depicted with dark blue skin and fiery hair, drinking blood from a cup made from a human skull, and riding side-saddle on either a mule or a mythological snow lion. She was said to be married to an evil king who raised their son to kill Buddhists. She tried many times to convert the king to Buddhism and end his hatred but was unsuccessful, and eventually she chose to kill their son while the king was out on a hunting trip. She then flayed him to use his skin as a saddle and drank his blood from a cup made of his own skull. She saddled a mule (or snow lion, depending on which version you read) and escaped north. Upon the king's return and finding his son massacred, he tried to shoot her with an arrow but missed and it pierced the hide of the mule or snow lion instead, which was subsequently healed by her and turned into an eye, so that it could watch over the twenty-four regions she had sworn to protect.

When she died in the mountains, she was reborn in hell and had to fight her way out, stealing a sack full of diseases and a sword on the way, as one does. When she escaped back to the charnel plane, she prayed to the Vajradhara to give her a reason to live (this Vajradhara is the ultimate primordial Buddha in several schools of Tibetan Buddhism). The Buddha asked her to protect the dharma – although there is no direct translation for the word into any Western tongue, it is roughly understood to be the sacred conduct and spiritual rules for humans to exist in cosmic harmony with the universe, and is the central concept of Buddhism. At this point, she was reborn as a dharmapāla (a wrathful god who protects the dharma) and is the only female deity among the traditional 'eight guardians of the law'.

The snow lion, known as a seng in the Indigenous language, which Palden Lhamo is sometimes depicted riding, is one of the four core mythological animals that appear in Vajrayāna Buddhism found in Bhutan. Although the snow lion is best known as the celestial symbol of Tibet you will also see it here, carved into buildings in beautiful bright colours against the contrast of its white skin. The snow lion is said to be the reincarnated embodiment of the joy and playfulness of Ānanda, one of the Buddha's ten disciples. They are said to exist in perpetual happiness and exuberance, and although they cannot fly, their feet never touch the ground as they leap from peak to peak in the mountains, endlessly.

This is, again, a reason why people are not permitted to scale the legendary Gangkhar Puensum mountain.

To best understand why Bhutan reveres these many mythological creatures so dearly, it is important to understand what they represent and the cosmological and epiphenomenal concepts they embody. Creatures in Western cultures are often feared and hunted – if you recall the entry on the Skinwalker Ranch in America (page 72), we saw that creatures from Native American belief systems were feared to be attacking other animals and scaring visitors to the ranch, that they are treated as being evil and vicious and people seek to hunt them down. But the actual people of the Indigenous tribes from whose belief systems these creatures came forth interpret them differently and do not want to discuss their lore with outsiders.

You can see how the same principles apply here, as many Westerners would no doubt deeply question why Bhutan has a wildlife reserve for the yeti or *mogai*, and why they do not permit mountaineering due to the peaks being considered the domain of deities and the *seng* or snow lion. They would likely insist on setting up watch stations with designs to capture or kill one of these creatures, because Western ideology places the self at the top of the food-chain, with everything else to be conquered. We can see this in the contrast between America having dozens of paranormal TV shows about hunting cryptids and Bhutan having a wildlife sanctuary for one.

The 'four auspicious beasts' of Buddhism each correspond to a point in a person's life cycle and a set of qualities that one must strive to achieve. We know about the snow lion and the thunder dragon but here you will also find the tiger and the garuda (a bird-like creature with a serpent in its grasp). The dragon (*druk*) represents power and awareness, the snow lion (*seng*) represents joy and fearlessness, the tiger (*tak*) represents confidence and overcoming adversity, and the garuda (*chung*) represents wisdom and achieving freedom. You'll see all four of these magnificent beasts displayed on the multi-coloured prayer flags found all over the country; they are also honoured with carved wooden masks of their faces, worn during the popular Tshechu festivals.

Regardless of your belief in any of these beasts as corporeal beings, what they symbolize in the minds of the people here and how they impact their society is undeniable. Many people view mythological creatures as simple fairytales for people who are not educated enough but is that just showing ignorance of the true meaning of such beliefs? At the core of the human experience lies our ability to make sense of our own existence by embodying difficult concepts into material or bodily forms. Belief is not always literal, and yet it is always powerful. When we believe, we make real that which we give power to. You can believe or not believe that the happy snow lion bounds from snow peak to snow peak in the towering Gangkhar Puensum mountain without ever touching the ground. Regardless, the mountain remains closed so you will not disturb it.

PREVIOUS LEFT: Tiger's Nest temples of the Taktsang Monastery.
PREVIOUS RIGHT: Gangkhar Puensum (White Peak of the Three Spiritual Brothers) is the holy mountain of Bhutan and is the highest unclimbed mountain (7571 m) on earth.

Acknowledgements

With thanks to the team at Quarto for the opportunity to put this atlas together; namely Richard, Phoebe, Bella, Daisy and Izzy. Team Conan — especially Louise, Rob, Jose. With honourable mention to my pub dad, Ritchie, who has always supported everything I do. My oldest friend Andrew for never giving up on me, my best friend Tiana for being the woman I hope to do right by, Connolly for being my shared husband and McHale for the fireworks. My late father for being too weird to live, my sister for always making me laugh, my mother for answering the starter for ten and my paternal grandparents for seeing that I got to where I needed to be. To Danny & Ciaran for always doing this weird stuff with me. WC Baer for bestowing me the supreme title of 'muse'.

For the late night freaks of Banshees, Bannermans, Opium, Studio 24, La Belle, and Uno Mas. Especially the team behind *Decade*; look at us now! For the film guys. For all the after parties. For the vampires that never die. And most importantly, thanks to the professor who told me Parapsychology was 'career suicide' — never been busier, babe.

Slàinte Mhath!

Picture Credits

14 Carol Di Rienzo Cornwell / Alamy Stock Photo; 16 Beata Chroniak / Alamy Stock Photo; 18-9 scenicireland.com / Christopher Hill Photographic / Alamy Stock Photo; 22 ColsTravel / Alamy Stock Photo; 23 Tom MacConnol; 27 a EWY Media / Shutterstock; 27 r Mark Summerfield / Alamy Stock Photo; 30 Borgvattnet's Parsonage; 31 Borgvattnet's Parsonage; 34 mrinalpal / Shutterstock; 35 travelview / Shutterstock; 38 Media Drum World / Alamy Stock Photo; 38 Media Drum World / Alamy Stock Photo; 40-1 Copyright © Andrew Nicholson, Virtual Tours of Scotland; 42-3 Universal History Archive / Getty Images; 46 t Ingus Kruklitis / Alamy Stock Photo; 46 b Wirestock Creators / Shutterstock; 50 AmityPhotos / Alamy Stock Photo; 51 Winchester Mystery House; 56 AU Photos / Alamy Stock Photo; 60 Xavier Campuzano Lopez / Shutterstock; 62 imagegallery2 / Alamy Stock Photo; 63 imagegallery2 / Alamy Stock Photo; 64-5 Aleksandr Ozerov / Shutterstock; 69 t Jon Arnold Images Ltd / Alamy Stock Photo; 69 b Wikimedia Commons; 72 Ronaldo Schemidt / AFP via Getty Images; 73 NEITPIX / Shutterstock; 76-7 Christina Simons / Alamy Stock Photo; 80 www.pqpictures.co.uk / Alamy Stock Photo; 81 Milosz Kubiak / Shutterstock; 82 l + r Chronicle / Alamy Stock Photo; 84-5 John Davidson Photos / Alamy Stock Photo; 90 SC Image / Shutterstock; 91 Backyard Productions / Alamy Stock Photo; 94-5 flocu / Shutterstock; 98 NaughtyNut / Shutterstock; 99 Sakdawut Tangtongsap / Shutterstock; 103 a Nick Ashdown; 103 b Fırat Aygün; 106 Leksi.photo / Shutterstock; 108 Alfredo Garcia Saz / Alamy Stock Photo; 109 AMIR MAKAR / Getty Images; 110-11 John Dambik / Alamy Stock Photo; 116 Peter Vanco / Shutterstock; 117 Peter Vanco / Shutterstock; 118 Apic / Bridgeman via Getty Images; 120-1 Egeris / Alamy Stock Photo; 124 a aeroviento / Flickr; 124 b aeroviento / Flickr; 125 aeroviento / Flickr; 128 Richard Newton / Alamy Stock Photo; 132–133 Richard Newton / Alamy Stock Photo; 136 SCStock / Shutterstock; 137 United Archives GmbH / Alamy Stock Photo; 140 a Kim Petersen / Alamy Stock Photo; 140 b Niels Quist / Alamy Stock Photo; 144-5 nearnights / Shutterstock; 150 Thomas H. Mitchell / Getty Images; 151 R. Nieuwland / Getty Images; 154 The_Evenesce_Photographer / Alamy Stock Photo; 155 Historic Collection / Alamy Stock Photo; 158-9 Carl Court / Getty Images; 162 imageBROKER.com GmbH & Co. KG / Alamy Stock Photo; 163 Matyas Rehak / Alamy Stock Photo; 166 Paolo Costa / Shutterstock; 167 mauritius images GmbH / Alamy Stock Photo; 170-1 PixelSenses / Shutterstock; 174 t Christopher M. Bartel / University of Maryland Art Gallery; 174 b Andrii Kozlytskyi / Getty Images; 178-9 FREEDOM_WANTED / Alamy Stock Photo; 182-3 Bihrmann / Shutterstock; 186 t ROGER NORMAN / Alamy Stock Photo; 186 b Ingo Oeland / Alamy Stock Photo; 192 GRANGER - Historical Picture Archive / Alamy Stock Photo; 193 Causeway Coast and Glens Museum Services; 196-7 Causeway Coast and Glens Museum Services; 200 Wirestock, Inc. / Alamy Stock Photo; 201 Frankris / Shutterstock; 204-5 Tang Yan Song / Shutterstock; 208-9 SW arts / Shutterstock; 212 t ullstein bild Dtl. / Getty Images; 212 b DmyTo / Shutterstock; 216 maodoltee / Shutterstock; 217 Mathias Putze / Alamy Stock Photo

Index

Quarto

First published in 2024 by Ivy Press,
an imprint of The Quarto Group.
One Triptych Place
London, SE1 9SH,
United Kingdom
T (0)20 7700 6700
www.Quarto.com

Design Copyright © 2024 Quarto
Text Copyright © 2024 Evelyn Hollow
Foreword Copyright © Danny Robins

Evelyn Hollow has asserted her moral right to be identified as the Author of
this Work in accordance with the Copyright Designs and Patents Act 1988.

All rights reserved. No part of this book may be reproduced or utilised in
any form or by any means, electronic or mechanical, including photocopying,
recording or by any information storage and retrieval system, without permission
in writing from Ivy Press.

Every effort has been made to trace the copyright holders of material quoted in
this book. If application is made in writing to the publisher, any omissions will
be included in future editions.

A catalogue record for this book is available from the British Library.

ISBN 978-0-7112-8796-9
Ebook ISBN 978-0-7112-8798-3

10 9 8 7 6 5 4 3 2 1

Publisher: Richard Green
Design: Daisy Woods
Editors: Bella Skertchly and Phoebe Bath
Editorial Assistant: Izzy Toner
Cartography: Martin Brown
Production Controller: Eliza Walsh

Printed in Malaysia